IN STEEL-GREY
ARMOUR

By

DAVID KER

W. & R. CHAMBERS LIMITED
LONDON AND EDINBURGH

CONTENTS

IN STEEL-GREY ARMOUR.

CHAPTER I.

BATTLING WITH THE FLOOD.

AFTERNOON was just waning into evening above the hill-tops of Northern Switzerland, on a raw, gusty, spring day about the middle of the thirteenth century, when a young knight came riding slowly and thoughtfully, all alone, over one of the dark, wooded ridges that followed each other in endless succession, like surging waves, all the way from the Aar to the Rhine.

As he crowned the ridge, he paused a moment ere descending to cast a long, wistful look at the spot where, far to the right, the tall, square tower of an ancient castle rose grey and sombre, on the rocky crest of the Wulpelsberg, against the gloomy April sky. 'Farewell, old tower!' he murmured, waving his hand toward it. 'God

only knoweth when I shall come back to
thee, or if I shall ever come back at all;
but I am in His hand, alike at home and
abroad.'

Young as he was (for his beard was hardly
grown yet), the speaker had evidently seen
something already of the cares and troubles
of life. There was a lurking sadness in
his handsome face, and on the high brow
over which curled his fair hair, was stamped
more than one deep furrow; but the frank,
fearless light in his clear blue eye told that
the simple manliness of the good old Swiss
stock from which he sprang was not lacking
to him.

Any practised observer would have known
him at a glance for one of those poverty-
stricken nobles who then swarmed in every
part of Central Europe. To begin with, he
was quite alone, whereas no man of rank
ever thought of stirring abroad in those days
without at least a dozen armed followers at
his back. Moreover, his armour, though
strong and workman-like, had not a sign of
that costly, showy ornament which was one
of the vices of the age; and his whole equip-
ment was so plain that even an ordinary
man-at-arms would have looked quite gay
beside him.

All at once, just as he was turning to go down the farther slope, a wild cry, as of one in mortal pain or terror, came to him from below in the direction of the rushing stream that foamed and roared at the base of the ridge.

The most natural explanation was that some one was being robbed and murdered, either by brigands or by the savage followers of those ferocious barons who were brigands in all but the name; and no ordinary man would have given a second thought to what was, in that lawless age, a mere everyday matter. But not so the brave young Swiss. For him it was enough that some one needed help; and his own imminent risk of being murdered if he interfered never checked him for an instant.

The next moment he was dashing down the steep, winding, slippery bridle-path at a speed that few riders would have dared to risk in such a place. But his gallant horse bore him safely to the foot of the perilous descent, where a startling sight awaited him.

The stream, usually so shallow and easily crossed, was rushing down in a foaming, roaring flood, which, swollen by the early melting of the snows and the torrent-rain of the last few days, was whirling away broken timbers, bundles of straw, up-torn bushes, and even whole trees.

Just then the cry for help was raised once more in the shrill, strained tones of utter desperation; but, look as he might, he could see no one. All at once, however, he espied on the bank (hidden till then by a clump of brushwood) an old man dressed as a monk, lying exhausted on the earth, deadly pale, and dripping water from every fold of his long grey robe.

'Hast thou indeed passed that wild water, father?' asked the young man in amazement.

'Nay, my son, I have but tried and failed,' panted the monk. 'Beyond this stream lieth one at point of death, to whom I am bearing the sacrament; and rather would I perish in yon flood than he should lack comfort in his last hour. Help me, as thou art knight and Christian!'

'That will I, right gladly,' cried the young knight, with a deeper flush on his bold handsome face; and, leaping from the saddle, he raised the old man's meagre frame in his strong arms like a child, set him on the horse, and, warning him to hold fast, led the noble beast right down into the raging flood.

At the first plunge he was all but whirled off his feet, strong as he was; and his good steed had to plant all its four hoofs firmly to save itself from being borne down by the fierce rush of the flood. But for the strong arm that upheld him, the feeble monk would have been hurled from the saddle like a stone out of a sling; and even the stalwart young noble was sorely pressed to hold his own, as the pitiless flood battered and tore at him like a living foe, beating on his breast-plate, lashing his horse's panting flank, and all but wrenching the trembling monk from his protector's hold.

Step by step he fought his way on; but how long could such a struggle last? Already the deadly chill of the ice-torrent was fast paralysing horse and man; and they were not yet half-way across, while the water was growing deeper and deeper every moment.

Even the brave young Swiss felt that, if they failed for one instant to find footing, they were lost; and all at once (as if to make their perilous case utterly hopeless) a huge pine-trunk came sweeping down on them with a rush like the shock of a battering-ram.

On, on swept the ponderous mass, one

blow of which would have crushed them like
flies; but just as all seemed over, its course
was suddenly arrested, and then it was seen
to swing round 'broadside-on' to the stream,
breaking the force of the current so greatly
that the exhausted men felt as if a strangling
clutch had been suddenly taken from their
throats.

'It is the hand of God!' said the pious
Swiss devoutly. 'We are saved.'

The next moment explained the seeming
miracle. The knight suddenly saw his horse
rise above him as if lifted bodily out of the
water; and one desperate struggle placed
him beside it on a jutting rock-ledge that at
this point formed a natural causeway beneath
the water, and on which the boughs of the
drifting pine had evidently caught.

Once in shallower water, the rest was
easy; and a minute more brought them safe
to land. For a time both were too much
spent to utter a word; and the monk was
the first to break silence. 'Yonder is the
hut whither I am bound, and, God be
praised, I am still in time. I thank thee,
my son; thou hast indeed done the part of
a Christian man.'

'And take my horse to bear thee home,
father,' said the knight earnestly; 'for since

he hath borne a servant of God and the holy
sacrament, it is not meet that he return to
the service of a sinner like me. Take him
as my free gift, and welcome.'

'I thank thee, son,' said the monk with
a slight smile, 'but methinks yon high-
mettled charger, which even thy strong hand
can barely curb, were an ill gift for a frail
old man who hath no skill to ride. Keep
thy goodly steed, my son, and may he bear
thee well; and if thou dost thy duty as a
true knight, to redress wrong and defend the
weak and helpless, he will assuredly be in
God's service as much with thee as with me.
And now tell me thy name, that I may bless
thee ere we part.'

'RUDOLF OF HAPSBURG,' said the young
hero, little dreaming that the still unknown
name which he uttered so modestly was one
day to be famed through the whole world,
and to write itself for ever in history.

'May God be with Rudolf of Hapsburg
now and henceforth,' said the old man
solemnly, as he laid his thin, trembling hand
on the kneeling youth's bowed head, around
which the sinking sun appeared to cast a
crown of gold. 'Be thou blessed, my son,
wherever thou goest; and as thou hast
humbled thyself to aid the meanest of God's

servants, so may He one day exalt thee higher than the highest!'

But how soon, and how strangely, that prophecy was to be fulfilled, neither the speaker nor the hearer, nor any other man living, could then have divined.

CHAPTER II.

THE RED-HAIRED BRIGAND.

WAVING his hand in farewell to the good monk, the Knight of Hapsburg rode briskly away; for, hardy as he was, he began to feel the effect of his super-human efforts and his long immersion in the icy stream. He felt he had no time to lose in reaching some place where he could be dried and warmed, and obtain the rest that he so much needed.

A village, he knew, lay but a few miles ahead, and toward it he hastened; but he reached it only to find himself confronted with a spectacle which, fatally common as it was in that iron age, startled and shocked even him.

The whole hamlet was one mass of smouldering ruins, from which a cloud of thick black smoke curled sullenly up against the grey, lowering sky. Charred beams, roofless walls, broken doors, half-burned timbers standing gauntly up out of heaps of still glowing ashes; and amid the wreck lay more than one corpse, as if some of the victims had died in a vain attempt to defend their plundered homes.

'Here be goodly doings in a Christian land!' said the young noble, with a frown of manly and righteous indignation at the horrible sight. 'Were I the emperor, methinks I would keep better order in my realm than to let mine own people be thus harried and slain in open day like wolves or wild swine!'

Just then a faint groan caught his ear; and, springing from his horse, he flew in the direction of the sound.

Half-buried beneath the ruin of a small hut lay the ragged, wasted form of a peasant woman with a young child in her arms, as if she had been struck down while striving to defend it. Perceiving some faint signs of life in both, the young man set himself to recall them to consciousness, and soon had the satisfaction of seeing the mother open her eyes. 'Food, food, for pity's sake,' she moaned faintly.

Rudolf drew a piece of bread from his pouch, and, crumbling it, moistened it with a few drops from his flask, and, bit by bit, saw it swallowed eagerly by mother and child, who seemed greatly revived by the knight's ministrations.

'How cam'st thou into this ill plight, good woman?' asked he pityingly.

'Our village was burned and plundered this morn,' she said faintly, 'by the men-at-arms of the Baron of Geierfels. Why he dealt thus with us I know not, for we never did him harm; but when the great ones fall out, whoever wins, we poor folks are sure to suffer.'

Rudolf winced as if stung, realising for the first time in what light he and his brother-nobles were viewed by the mass of the people; but he controlled himself, and asked gently if she had any friend with whom she could take refuge.

'I have a cousin, noble sir,' said she, 'among the good sisters of the convent of St Ursula at Bruck; and, can I but reach them, I doubt not but they will give me shelter.'

'It is a long way, and thou wilt be hard put to it to fare thither with thy child in this stormy weather,' said the knight kindly. 'Little have I to give, but, such as it is, it is freely thine.'

He emptied his meagre purse into her lap, and, amid a shower of incoherent bless-

ings, turned and rode away. But it seemed
as if his generous aid had been given in
vain; for hardly was he gone, when from
the thicket behind peered out several grim
and brutal faces, and five ruffianly fellows
(ragged and filthy, but all armed to the
teeth) came stealing forth.

'Hand over quickly what yon threadbare
knight gave thee,' said the foremost robber
to the trembling woman, with a savage
laugh. 'We are the leviers of tolls on
this highway, and suffer none to pass toll-
free.'

'And think not to trick us by hiding
any away,' growled a second, 'or it may
go ill with that brat of thine, who shall
presently try if his head or yon post be
the harder.'

He seized the screaming child as if to
carry out his horrid threat at once, while
the distracted mother shrieked for aid,
though with little hope of obtaining it.
But her cries, ringing through the deep
silence of the fast-falling night, reached the
quick ear of Rudolf, who was not yet out
of hearing; and there was still light enough
for him, as he wheeled his horse, to take
in the whole scene at a glance. The sight
of these villains wresting from the forlorn

and homeless outcast her last hope of life kindled the young noble's bold blood to fire; and, couching his lance, he came upon the ruffians like a thunderbolt.

Two of the robbers were dashed to the earth, stunned and senseless, by the mere shock of the charging war-horse; and Rudolf's lance smote a third full on the chest, and went right through him from breast to back. The two others fell upon him like tigers; but he, dropping his entangled lance, laid the nearest man dead with one sword-stroke.

The fifth bandit, however (seemingly the leader of the ruffianly gang), was not so easily disposed of. He was a short, bull-necked, red-haired man, plainly of immense strength; and the skill with which he wielded his halberd (a formidable weapon like a spear and battle-axe in one) showed him to be a practised fighter.

He evidently meant to kill or maim the knight's horse, a mishap which, to a cavalier of that day, was second only to the loss of his own life. Fearing for his good steed, and being at a disadvantage against his foe's longer weapon, Hapsburg sprang from his saddle to assail the bandit at close quarters; but he instantly found his arms

pinned to his sides by a clutch as terrible
as the hug of a bear.

With a last effort the young warrior
wrenched his right hand free, and, having
no room for the sweep of his sword, he
dealt the robber a terrific blow on the
temple with its heavy pommel, beating him
down to the earth as if crushed by a falling
rock.

And then, as the bandit lay senseless at
his feet, there awoke in the young Switzer's
gallant heart a great pity for this man who
had fought so well in a bad cause. Almost
any other man of that cruel age would
have cut the robber's throat on the spot,
and gone on as unheedingly as if he had
only crushed a gnat; but Rudolf's natural
kindness of heart, roused to the utmost by
the old monk's heroic self-devotion and by
his own recent goodness to the forlorn
widow and her child, shrank from the very
thought of slaying a helpless foe. He
bathed the stunned man's face with water
from the brook, and ere long saw him open
his eyes and gaze around him with a
vacant stare, which suddenly changed to a
scowl of dogged defiance.

'Slay me, then, as I would have slain
you,' he growled, casting a look of wither-

ing scorn after his two surviving followers, who, the moment they came to their senses, had taken to their heels like the cowardly rogues they were. 'Slay me quickly; I ask no mercy!'

'Not I,' said Hapsburg; 'he who would strike a helpless man who cannot defend himself is no true knight.'

The robber eyed him in wondering silence, as if hardly able to believe a declaration so utterly opposed to his own experience and practice.

'Stand up on thy feet; I will not harm thee,' went on the knight, aiding him to rise. 'Never yet did man face me as stoutly as thou hast done, and methinks thou art too good to herd with such scum as yon curs who ran away but now.'

'Now, may Heaven reward you for that good word, Sir Knight,' cried the bandit, with a visible softening of his grim features; ''tis the first word of kindness I have heard for many a day!'

'And as thou canst feel it thus, thou art not yet wholly given over to evil,' said Rudolf heartily. 'Give me thy hand, good fellow, and tell me who and what thou art.'

'What?' cried the robber, drawing back

instinctively. 'Can a knight and a noble like yourself take the hand of such a one as I am?'

'Why not? Our Lord Himself touched lepers and heretics,' said the young noble, grasping his hand with a heartiness that could not be mistaken.

'God's blessing on your kind heart, noble sir,' said the robber in a tremulous voice. 'I deemed not there was a knight living this day who would give his hand in fellowship to one that is but a common robber, rightly named "Henkers-Knecht"' (Gallows-Lad), 'having well deserved the gallows many and many a time.'

'But now, please God, it shall be so no longer,' cried the knight, with a frank kindliness that went straight to the outcast's heart. 'Hear me, my friend. I go to Rheinfelden to join the host of King Ottocar of Bohemia, and march under his banner to defend our Christian brethren of East Prussia, who are sore pressed by the Wendish heathen. It is a good and righteous cause, as any crusade to Holy Land, and needeth just such men as thee to maintain it. Come with me, then, and be true henchmen to me, as I will be true lord to thee; and henceforward shalt thou be no more called Henkers-Knecht, but Andrer-Knecht' (Other Lad), 'for, with God's help, thou shalt indeed be another man from this day forth!'

The robber eagerly assented; and a few minutes later the Knight of Hapsburg was riding off again in the direction of Rhein-felden, with his strange recruit striding man-fully along by his side.

CHAPTER III.

FACING A GIANT.

OUR hero had but a poor chance of finding lodgings at his journey's end, for the little town of Rheinfelden, whither he was bound, was already full to the very doors. Every inn was crowded to overflowing, and not a few gentlemen of rank were sleeping in tents, or even under the open sky, along either bank of the river. This spring-tide of customers had reached even the outlying inns on the highway; and a party of seven merchants from Basel, who had just halted before the 'Golden Eagle,' three miles from Rheinfelden itself, looked manifestly doubtful as to what answer their application for food and lodging might receive.

'Fain would I pleasure you, Master Ellstock, or any of your worshipful trade,' said the host, with the civility due to a good customer; 'but if ye would bide here to-night ye must be content to lodge in the *Stube*' (public-room) 'and to bear with

my company there, for in mine own
chamber there be two lodgers already.'

'Content are we,' said the chief trader,
visibly relieved; for, in that lawless age, it
was no light risk to camp out after dark.
'As to our lads here,' added he, with a
glance at the fifteen stout fellows who stood
ready to unload and unsaddle the pack-
horses, 'they are not so dainty but what a
truss of straw in the stable will serve them
well, so they have but meat and drink
withal. And now tell us, I pray thee, what
news is stirring here beyond the muster
of King Ottocar's army, whereof we know
already.'

'If there be little to tell to-day, to-morrow
shall men have enow to gossip of,' said the
host, with the important air of one who had
something to tell worth hearing. 'Know
ye the Abbot of Reichenau?'

'Abbot Paulus? Who in these parts
knows him not? But what of him?'

'Marry, for some displeasure that he
hath given to King Ottocar, the king hath
granted him but seven days to find the
right answer to three questions that he
hath set him. To-morrow is the term out;
and if the abbot cannot then answer them
aright, he must be led through the town

on an ass, with his face to the tail, and put to open shame before all men.'

'That were ill done, so to mishandle a man of holy church on the eve of a march against the heathen,' said Ellstock, shaking his head. 'Little blessing can he look for, I trow, on an enterprise so begun. But tell me, good host, know'st thou what the three questions be?'

'Every child in Rheinfelden knows them, for nought else is talked of among us here; and right hard questions they be, in sooth. First must he say how much the king himself may be worth, wearing his crown and all his jewels. Then must he tell in how long a time a man may journey around the world; and, lastly, he must say aright what thought is in the king's own mind, and wherein that thought is wrong.'

'Hard questions, as thou say'st,' cried Ellstock; 'and methinks——'

But he was interrupted by a sudden and confused clamour of harsh voices outside the courtyard gate; and then came a roar like thunder: 'Ho there, dog of a host! come hither to me quickly!'

The poor host, thus roughly summoned, came forward with a cringing air, like a dog expecting to be beaten; he found himself amid a throng of armed men, and face to face with a black-bearded knight of huge stature and giant frame, whose inflamed features and bloodshot eyes told him that he was no stranger to that habitual intemperance which was the chief sin of the age. 'Hark ye, fellow,' he growled, 'my henchman saith he hath found all the inns of Rheinfelden choke-full; wherefore thou shalt lodge me and my train to-night, and look to it that we be well entertained, or woe to thy churl-carcass!'

The ill-starred host shook as he listened; for, by the vulture-crest on the speaker's helmet, he knew him as the dreaded Baron of Geierfels, the most brutal and pitiless of those robber-lords that were the pest of Rhineland, who had (as already seen) destroyed a whole village only the day before in a fit of drunken fury. 'Glad, indeed, would I be, noble sir,' faltered he, 'to have the honour of harbouring you; but here is no such entertainment as befits your worship, and, moreover, every corner of my poor house——'

'Is full, thou wouldst say?' roared the baron. 'What care I? Turn out these lodgers of thine, be they who they may; and if one man be left in the house when

I enter it, my men-at-arms shall hurl him
from the window! Deemest thou, rogue,
that I am one to be turned from thy door
like a stray dog, for the sake of a rabble
of pedlars like these?'

An angry murmur broke from the affronted
traders, not a little indignant at being so
insolently expelled from the shelter that
they had just secured. But it died away
at once as Geierfels sprang from his horse
and threw open the visor of his helmet; for
they all knew him to their cost.

'Have mercy, noble baron!' pleaded the
host, falling on his knees. 'For myself I
ask no favour; but, for God's sake, have
pity on my aged father, who lieth here sore
sick, and may not be moved without peril
of his life.'

'A curse on thy father and thee too!'
roared the savage, spurning the suppliant
from him. 'If he be like to die, let him;
'tis time, an' he be old and useless. No
more words, but clear me the house straightway, else will I fire this kennel of thine at
all four corners at once; and who shall dare
to gainsay me?'

'*I* will,' said a quiet but firm voice at
his side, so unexpectedly that all looked
round with a start; and their amazement

rose higher still when they saw from whom
this bold defiance came.

Right in the blustering noble's path stood
a slim, graceful form in shining steel, whose
open helmet showed a smooth, ruddy, boyish
face, which any Italian artist would have
loved to paint in the ranks of a choir of
cherubs.

'They have taken thee from thy nurse
too soon, child,' said Geierfels, with a
savage sneer. 'What hast *thou* to do
among bearded men?'

'Only to beat some courtesy into a black
bear that hath been growling somewhat too
loud,' retorted the new-comer, looking full
in the swaggerer's coarse face with a glance
of withering scorn. 'I, who am knight and
noble, may well gainsay a ruffian who hath
disgraced the name of both; and I call
upon all true men who hear me, in the
name of our lord the king, to stand by me
in protecting this honest man from violence!'

'Here is one who will,' said a clear voice
from behind, as a knight in steel-grey
armour, followed by a stout, red-haired man
with a long halberd, ranged himself beside
the young champion and his two attendants.

'And here be other some that will do
the like,' added Ellstock the trader, whose

bold German blood was fairly up at the robber-baron's insolence. 'Up with right and justice, and down with all brawlers and swashbucklers, whoe'er they be!'

The enraged bully's first impulse was to bid his men-at-arms fall on and butcher the 'base churls' who dared to oppose his will; but one glance told him what his wavering followers had already perceived, that this would be no safe or easy task. Having sent on most of his men to the camp, and kept only a few as his personal guard, his present train (including himself and two esquires) numbered but thirty-three. On the other hand, the merchants and their men were twenty-two, all well armed; and the two young knights, with their three henchmen, made up twenty-seven, while there could be no doubt which side the inn-servants and village folk (who were already crowding in) would take in a fray provoked by the insolence of one so universally hated as himself.

Ruffian as he was, Geierfels was no fool, and saw at once that his favourite method of brute force would not do here; for who could tell but what this youth might be a friend of the king to whom he had appealed so boldly, or how King Ottocar

(who had special reasons just then to con-
ciliate the Rhineland folk) might view such
an outrage?

But the baron saw, too, another way by
which, in a manner universally approved
by that age, he could at least wreak his
vengeance on the presumptuous stripling
who had defied him. 'Is thy heart as bold
as thy tongue, boy?' asked he jeeringly,
'or art thou all words and no deeds? Dar'st
thou cope with me here, man to man?'

'Be this my answer!' cried the youth, as
he tore the steel gauntlet from his hand,
and dashed it with such force in his
challenger's savage face as to draw blood
from the bearded cheek.

'Thy life shall pay for that insolence!'
roared the giant, drawing his sword. 'Look
to thyself, for I will give thee no mercy!'

'I ask none,' was the calm reply.

'Form up, and keep the ground clear!
cried he of the steel-grey armour, in a tone
of authority. 'This is a fair field, and
whoso disturbs it, dies by my hand!'

The men-at-arms silently obeyed; for the
unheard-of daring of these two young
strangers had begun to impress them all
with a vague, superstitious awe.

'Think'st thou not, comrade,' whispered

one, 'that yon youth is strangely like unto the blessed St Michael in the church at Rheinfelden?'

'His very image,' said the other, crossing himself with a shudder; 'and methinks he *can* be no mortal champion, or he durst not have defied our master, who hath never met his match in fight.'

Ere another word could be spoken, the giant's sword rose and fell with the rush of a whirlwind, and the young man sprang aside barely in time to escape. A second stroke flashed right at his neck, and the lookers-on drew a quick breath, expecting to see his head swept from his shoulders. A sudden bound backward foiled the blow, but it came so near that the plume was shorn from his helmet, and floated away into the air.

But, to the more experienced spectators, the fight seemed not so unequal after all; for, in spite of the difference in strength and size, a heavy man of forty-five, unstrung by habitual excess, might well find his match in an active lad of twenty, toughened by constant exercise, and temperate as a hermit.

'David and Goliath,' muttered Ellstock with a grim chuckle, glancing from the

black-bearded giant to his ruddy, boyish
foe.

It seemed as if he were right; for though,
for a few moments, all the youth's marvellous agility could barely keep him unharmed
amid that storm of crashing blows (the least
of which seemed able to cleave a solid rock),
it was not long ere the baron's strokes
began to fall less fiercely, his lips to quiver
convulsively, and his labouring breath to
come in hoarse gasps.

Feeling his strength failing, he growled a
savage curse, and swung up his terrible
blade for a decisive blow; but as he did
so, the violence of his movements made an
opening between his shoulder-plate and the
steel 'rere-brace' on his upper arm. Quick
as thought, in flashed the stranger's point,
and a red stain on the shining steel showed
that the thrust had not been vain.

Geierfels bellowed like a wild bull with
pain and fury, and thundered a blow on
him that might have beaten down a wall.
There was a loud clang—a general cry—
and the stranger's helmet flew half across
the courtyard, leaving him bareheaded before
his merciless foe.

'God help him!' muttered the innkeeper,
turning away his face.

Well might he say so, for the giant's next blow fell like a thunderbolt, cutting right through the youth's left vambrace, and beating him down on his knees with the sheer weight of the stroke. The men-at-arms set up a hoarse shout of triumph, and Geierfels, with the grin of a demon, rushed in to make an end of his seemingly helpless foe; but ere he could strike, the other leaped to his feet again, and assailed him at close quarters. Their swords became entangled, and a sharp crash was suddenly heard, as the claw-shaped hilt of the baron's weapon caught his opponent's blade, and snapped it short off!

A quick gasp of terror broke from the gazing villagers, as they saw the giant's cruel steel quiver above the bright young head that it was raised to cleave in twain. But ere it could fall, the Unknown, with his broken blade, gave him a dreadful slash in the face, laying it open from brow to chin; and down toppled the Goliath like a falling tower, and lay motionless on the earth.

'What means this?' asked a stern commanding voice amid the dead hush of blank amazement that followed; and the spectators, looking round with a start, saw

to their dismay that the richly dressed
cavalier who had just ridden up with a
numerous train at his back was King Ottocar
himself!

The steel-grey knight, prompt as ever,
told the story in a few simple, straight-
forward words. 'And should this man
survive the blow,' he added emphatically,
'he shall underlie my challenge, as a felon
knight and a cowardly oppressor of the poor.'

'Well and knightly spoken!' cried the
king heartily; 'and right glad am I to see
that thou wearest my colours, for the cause
in which I march needs the arm of every
true knight. Who and whence art thou?'

'Rudolf of Hapsburg,' said our hero
modestly; 'a poor Swiss knight.'

'Rudolf of Hapsburg?' echoed the baron's
conqueror, stepping briskly forward. 'We
are cousins, then, for I am CONRAD OF
HOHENZOLLERN. Well met, cousin.'

The two young men grasped each other's
hands cordially, and the king eyed them
with an approving smile, though he little
dreamed that in these two unknown lads
who bowed to him so respectfully, he saw
the founder of a line of Austrian emperors,
and the ancestor of the future kaisers of a
united Germany.

'I am indeed in luck to-day,' said the great king with a good-humoured laugh. 'It is not every king, I trow, that hath in his ranks a champion who could overcome a swordsman like Geierfels, or a knight who could stand by him for justice' sake against thirty men-at-arms. Come back with me to the town, both of you; and on the morrow, when I sit in judgment on the Abbot of Reichenau, see that ye be both present in the hall.'

CHAPTER IV.

THE KING'S THREE QUESTIONS.

ON the next morning, the town of Rheinfelden (already quite full enough) was fairly overflowed by a noisy and excited crowd; for the news of the king's displeasure against the Abbot of Reichenau, the three strange questions set him by Ottocar, and the public disgrace awaiting him if he failed to answer them, had run through the whole district, and every one was eager to see how he would come off.

'For a plain man such questions are indeed too deep,' said a burly peasant from the other bank of the Rhine, 'but for a scholar and a churchman it were surely no hard matter to find the right answer thereto.'

'Marry, I would not be too sure of that,' chuckled a sun-browned pedlar, with his pack on his back. 'The abbot is a good man, none better; but it is no sacrilege, I trow, to say what I have heard the brethren of Reichenau say themselves, that his heart is stronger than his head.'

'True,' said a brawny smith, shrugging his shoulders; 'if ever he go to Schiltburg' (the town of fools) 'he may fairly claim the rights of a free burgher there.'

'Well, be he wise or no, I wish him well out of it,' put in a stout, ruddy market-woman; 'for he hath ever been good to the poor.'

In another corner of the market-place, two of Geierfels's men-at-arms were startling some of their cronies with the tale of their master's defeat by the stranger, which, as may be supposed, lost nothing in the telling.

'I saw it with my own eyes, lads, as plain as I see you now,' cried one, 'and I have not slept a wink for thinking on 't. It was the blessed St Michael himself, even as he stands limned' (painted) 'in yon church-window above us; and by him stood St George in steel-grey armour, and defied the whole thirty of us at once!'

'Ye know how our master can smite,' added the other; 'but all his blows fell as vainly as if he wielded a bulrush in place of a sword, and at the last he was smitten down as if Heaven's lightning fell on him. Then, when the king came up, St George spake to him and told the tale, and forthwith, before the eyes of all men, both the heavenly ones vanished away!'

His hearers listened eagerly, believing every word; for, to any man of that age, it was not only possible but quite natural that an angel should come down from heaven, in bodily form, to punish the presumption of a mortal. But just then their talk was broken by a loud blast of trumpets, and King Ottocar himself, with a glittering train of knights and nobles, came riding along the narrow, crowded street.

The great Bohemian ruler was a man in the prime of life, of noble bearing and powerful frame, and looking 'every inch a king,' as, in truth, he was, ere pride and prosperity had combined to warp his better nature.

Among those around him were several men whose names are now written in history. There appeared the portly form and clear grey eye of the great Archbishop of Maintz; and the young Duke of Swabia's tall slim figure and handsome boyish face; and red-bearded, scowling Count Valens of Thuringia, a cousin of the Baron of Geierfels, and as great a ruffian as his kinsman; and the sleek, courteous, ever-smiling Cardinal Malaspina, the Pope's legate, come to bless this new crusade against the 'Prussian heathen.'

Amid this jungle of plumed hats and shining lace, no one but the king himself (who greeted them with a friendly wave of his hand as he entered the town-hall) took any notice of two such humble persons as Sir Conrad of Hohenzollern and Sir Rudolf of Hapsburg, who were standing modestly by the door. Had a seer or astrologer suddenly announced to that brilliant company that this quiet young Swiss was the greatest man of them all, one can fancy with what incredulous scorn his words would have been received; yet such was the case, though they little dreamed of it, and he himself least of all.

King Ottocar placed himself on the 'seat of state' (a huge, solid chair of carved oak) and awaited the abbot's coming; nor had he long to wait. Hardly had the last of his train been marshalled to their places in the hall, when the measured chant of a Latin hymn was heard coming nearer and nearer, and then came a shout from the guards at the door: 'Make way there! make way for the lord abbot of Reichenau!'

In through the shadowy archway swept

a tall figure in high mitre and flowing
robes; but in place of being attended by
a numerous train (like all dignitaries of
that age, church or lay), the abbot's only
followers were six dark-robed monks.

The courtiers exchanged looks of surprise, and the king himself seemed in
doubt whether to regard this unwonted
humility as a compliment or an affront.
He made no remark, however, and answered
only with a slight bend of his head the
abbot's solemn greeting of 'Pax vobiscum'
(peace be with you). 'Abbot of Reichenau,'
said he, 'we have set thee, as thou knowest,
three questions; art thou ready to answer
them?'

'I am,' said the abbot, in a tone which,
low as it was, sounded unnaturally loud
amid the dead hush of expectation that had
fallen suddenly over the crowded hall.

The king's look of surprise at this confident reply was mirrored in every other
face in the hall; not a few of those
present had themselves witnessed the abbot's
perplexity and dismay when this strange
task was first set him, and all alike fully
expected him to confess himself beaten,
and appeal to the king for mercy; but this
certainly did not look much like it.

'Tell me, then,' said Ottocar at last, 'how much I may be worth, wearing my crown and royal jewels?'

'Our Lord Himself was sold for thirty pieces of silver,' replied the abbot solemnly, 'and therefore, wear as many jewels as thou wilt, thou canst be worth no more than nine-and-twenty, for no mortal man can be rated at equal value with Him!'

A murmur of amazement buzzed through the crowd, and the king himself winced visibly, as if he felt this quiet but pointed rebuke to that overweening pride that was his chief fault, and was destined to cost him dear in after days. 'So far, well,' said he after a pause; 'but now tell me how long it may take a man to ride around the whole world.'

'If he ride in the car of the sun,' replied the abbot quietly, 'twenty-four hours should suffice him.'

This time there was an audible titter from the listeners, which even the awe of the royal presence could not wholly suppress; and the king himself looked fairly nonplussed. 'Thou hast a shrewder wit than I weened, lord abbot,' cried he, half-vexed and half-laughing; 'but methinks my third question will cast thee out of the saddle, though all the learning of the ancients hold thee up. Tell me, then, what is the thought in my mind even now, and is that thought right or wrong?'

'That will I do forthwith,' said the abbot, as calmly as ever. 'Thy thought is that I am the Abbot of Reichenau, and therein art thou in error, for I am but his shepherd, Hans Bendix.'

So saying, the pretended abbot whipped off his mitre, fully disclosing, for the first time, a face which, though so marvellously like the abbot's own that it might have misled even a close observer, was seen to be framed in the close-cropped hair which then distinguished a peasant from a noble.

At this unlooked-for turning of the tables, the general mirth could no longer be restrained, and the hall shook with a universal roar of laughter, in which the king himself joined heartily. Even the crowd outside (to whom the joke had been passed on by those who were near enough to the open door to hear it) echoed the laugh with a will, delighted at the idea of the king himself having been outwitted by a man of their own class.

'I wist not that the abbot had a double,' cried Ottocar, still laughing; 'truly thou

art marvellously like him, good fellow.
Well, since thou hast done what thy master
could not do, I make thee abbot this day
in his place.'

'What, I?' said Bendix, with a broad
grin. 'A choice abbot I should make, who
can neither read nor write; and even were
it otherwise, not to save my neck from the
hangman would I thrust my good master
from his place.'

'Thy *good* master, say'st thou?' cried
the king. 'Know'st thou that within this
very week he hath given *me* great cause of
displeasure?'

'The truth is the truth,' replied the
shepherd sturdily; 'and though I sorrow
as much as he that he hath displeased your
Majesty, I stand to it that (as all the poor
of this district can tell thee) there is no
man alive fit to fill his place!'

The courtiers looked aghast at this bold
contradiction; but the rough peasant's blunt
loyalty to his master went straight to the
gallant heart of King Ottocar, who, himself
one of the bravest men that ever lived, could
fully appreciate such courageous devotion.
'Thou art a good fellow, Hans Bendix,'
said he heartily, 'and I would that every
subject of mine were as loyal. Four rose-

nobles a year do I give thee henceforth, to cherish thy wit withal; and if thou hast a mind for adventure and advancement, come with me against the northern heathen.'

'That will I do blithely,' cried Hans, 'if my master the abbot permit; for without his leave, look you, I can do nothing.'

But the overjoyed abbot could refuse nothing to the man who had saved him, and, a week later, Hans Bendix, with the king's colours in his steel cap, was marching northward in the ranks of the royal army.

CHAPTER V.

A RACE FOR LIFE.

A WIDE, bare, sandy plain, the dreary sameness of which ended at last in a broad belt of rank, unwholesome green, betraying the presence of one of the fearful morasses that were then so formidably common along the desolate shores of the Baltic. A distant mass of black, shadowy woods framing the dismal scene; and, on the brow of a low ridge, or rather knoll, in the foreground, a strange-looking wooden building, battlemented and loop-holed, with a tall, square tower in its midst; and all around it (enclosing a large space of ground) a high, strong palisade of rough timber, girdled with a deep ditch brimful of water.

Sorely would it have startled the men who garrisoned that remote outpost (a tiny islet of human skill and valour and knowledge, in that sea of brutal heathen barbarism and unredeemed desolation) could they have beheld in a vision the future

history of the rude timber fort that they
had piously named 'Marien-Burg' (Mary's
Tower) and seen the thriving modern town
of Marienburg looking down on the smooth
east Prussian railway, along which so many
well-appointed trains go flying every day
to the Baltic States, to Poland, to Russia,
through what was then an unknown and
hideous wilderness.

But that band of stolid Swiss crossbowmen, hard-headed German men-at-arms,
and plain, sturdy Dutch emigrants, were too
fully occupied with the present to trouble
themselves about the future. Hemmed in
as they were by fathomless morasses, wolf-
haunted forests, and swarms of merciless
savages, their chief care just then was to
get to the end of each day with their
heads on their shoulders, and their shelter-
ing fort unburned.

At the narrow, loop-hole-like window of
a small chamber in the upper part of the
tower sat writing, just where he could
catch what little light struggled through
the leaden clouds of the grey, sullen evening sky, a man who, little as he himself
guessed it, was the beginner of a work of
which the world has not yet seen the
end.

He was a man of fine stature and power-ful frame, and still young in years, as might be seen by the elastic vigour of all his movements, and by the mute evidence of the ponderous two-handed sword in the corner behind him, and of the weighty helmet and breast-plate on the wall above. But the tell-tale streaks of grey in his crisp black hair, and the deep lines that furrowed his noble face, told that he had led no easy life.

Nor had he, in truth; for this man was the Hoch-meister (Grand Master) of the Knights of the Teutonic Brotherhood, Her-mann von der Salza, who had now been labouring for twenty years and more at one of the hardest tasks ever laid upon mortal man.

Half a century earlier, some kind-hearted Germans who had been swept into the whirl of Richard Cœur-de-Lion's disastrous Crusade, formed themselves into what we should now call a 'Nursing Society,' in aid of their ill-fated countrymen, who were dying like flies in the fatal climate of Syria. Up to the end of the Crusade, this was their sole employment; but by that time so many willing and capable men had joined them, that their chiefs decided to

form the association into a regularly organ-
ised brotherhood, on the model of the
Templars and the Knights of St John,
with the title of 'The Hospital Knights
of the German Brotherhood of St Mary.'

This was done, and the new Order, with
Venice for its headquarters, and brave
Walpot von Bassenheim ('a noble not by
birth but by deeds') for its first Grand
Master, had already existed twenty-five
years or so, when, one fine summer morning,
a way-worn messenger came wearily into
Venice inquiring for the new head of the
Order, Hermann von der Salza.

To the joyful surprise of Hermann (who
was growing weary of watching and waiting
for a new crusade that never came) that
messenger brought him an all-important
letter from a man as brave and devoted as
himself—the good prelate who was actual
Bishop of Riga and titular 'Bishop of
Prussia,' and had the care of the little
fringe of scattered Christian communities
that contrived to exist in the teeth of frost,
hunger, fever, floods, wild beasts, and blood-
thirsty savages along the dreary Baltic sea-
board.

Short as it was, that letter was very
much to the purpose, and fated to have

far greater results than either writer or
reader dreamed of; and this was what it
said:

'BROTHER AND DEAR FRIEND!—There is
ever work to be done in God's vineyard, and
when a man findeth it not in one corner
thereof, he will assuredly light on it in
another; and it befits not a man like thee,
the fame of whose good deeds have rejoiced
our ears even in this far-off land, to sit
with folded hands while the kingdom of
Satan is exalted.   Till it shall please
Heaven to stir up anew the zeal of our
princes, there is nought to be done against
the Saracen infidels of Holy Land; but
here, in this very land where I dwell, a
new crusade awaits thee and thy valiant
brethren—as noble a one as was e'er
achieved by kaiser or king.   Here be
Christian folk to defend against the heathen,
forests to fell, swamps to drain, rich lands
to redeem from the wilderness, foul idols
to break in pieces, the worship of the true
God to maintain and extend; wherefore I
say unto thee (even as the man of Mace-
donia said unto the apostle of old), "Come
over and help us!"'

Within two years from that day, the
grand-master and all his knights were

established in the heart of the wild 'No
Man's Land' between the Vistula and the
Niemen; and a new stage in the endless
battle of civilisation and barbarism was
fairly begun. What kind of work he and
his men had to do, and how they were
doing it, may be best gathered from the
letter that he was then writing to his friend
the Bishop:

'The heathen do yet press us sore, and
right welcome be the tidings which we have
lately gotten, that King Ottocar comes to
our aid with a great host. Howbeit, this
our new fortress of Marien-Burg standeth
well for our work, and I think to make it
mine headquarters, for from thence may I
most easily control the violence of the
heathen, and be as a wall betwixt them
and our quiet folk of the coast.

'The draining of the quagmires goeth
forward, albeit but slowly, the work being
so great and toilsome; but we have been
manfully helped therein by the Flanderkins
and Hollanders that be of our company,
who, being much practised of dyking and
embanking in their own land, are well able
to do us masterful service. Also we have
driven a causeway right athwart the morass
that lieth south and east of our burg, so

that now man and horse may fare forth
without risk to be swallowed up therein.

'Touching our bodily estate, we have lost
certain good and true men (on whose souls
may God have mercy) by the swamp-sickness,
which is ever most grievous in the summer-
time. Nor hath the winter been more kind
to us than the summer; for scarce was Yule-
tide past, when there fell so great and heavy
a snow, that it lay over man's height all
round our walls, so that none might adventure forth. Ill had it gone with us then,
had we not laid up great store of supplies;
howbeit our horses were scant of fodder ere
the change of the season set us free, and
the cold so increased upon us that no fire
might wholly overcome it.

'Nathless God hath been gracious unto
us, and hath granted us sundry mercies to
atone for these ill-haps. For it befell that
on Christmas Eve we came suddenly, but
two leagues hence, on certain priests of the
heathen who were sacrificing to their filthy
idols, and with them a great throng of worshippers; and, falling on them by surprise,
we slew all the common folk of them, and
the priests we burned with their idols; for
which mercy may Heaven be praised! That
same night we set forth again; and on

Christmas morn it was our good hap to light on another band of the idolaters, three hundred or more, whom we compassed about, and slew them every one!'

Such were the offerings that a Christian leader and a naturally kind-hearted man gave to the God of love and mercy at the season of universal peace and good-will! But in those days, unhappily, men as good and noble as the famous grand-master himself were wont to regard all non-Christian races, not as human beings with souls and bodies like themselves, but as weeds and briars cumbering God's earth, fit only to be cut down and cast into the fire; and we can hardly blame Hermann von der Salza for thinking and acting as all men, even the best, thought and acted in that savage and ignorant age.

Hardly were the last words traced on the parchment, when (as if to be in keeping with their grim suggestiveness) rang out overhead a long, shrill trumpet-blast, the usual signal of alarm.

Hermann sprang to his feet with all a soldier's promptitude; and as he did so, came pealing on the rising wind a yell so frightful and unearthly that even Von der Salza started slightly, used to it as he was. It

was the yell of the savage Wends of East
Prussia, which was to all the Christians of
that wild region what the Indian war-whoop
was in later times to the first settlers in
North America.

In a moment more the grand-master was
darting as nimbly as a boy up the steep,
narrow, ladder-like stair of the tower; and
as he came out on the small, square, battlemented platform at the top, a strange and
startling scene lay before him.

Far out on the great plain, a little beyond
where the dull grey of the barren sand began
to give place to the rank, ominous green of
the fatal morass, two men were seen running
as if for their lives; and well they might,
for close behind them came, with fierce
gestures and wolfish yells, a swarm of wild
figures (twenty at the least) who were evidently a band of the heathen savages whose
cruelties had made the name of 'Wend' a
by-word through all Europe.

The sunset gleam that broke just then
through the lowering sky showed both
fugitives to be fully clothed and armed;
and Hermann, jumping at once to the con-
clusion that they were either stragglers from
King Ottocar's advancing host, or messengers
sent to tell him of its near approach,

promptly ordered a sally to rescue them.
'Let your horses be, lads,' he cried; 'while
we are saddling and leading them out, yon
brave fellows may be slain. On foot and
shoulder to shoulder, like brothers!'

In a trice thirty well-armed men, with
Hermann himself at their head, were racing
at full speed toward the scene of action.
But all at once the grand-master's glowing
face was seen to cloud over, and from his
lips broke a muttered exclamation of dismay,
for which, in truth, there was but too good
reason.

CHAPTER VI.

ONE AGAINST TWENTY.

THE two hunted men had evidently caught sight of the raised causeway across the morass, and were making for it; but, most unluckily, the direction of their flight had brought them some way to the left of the point at which the causeway joined the firm ground, and to alter their course now would be to run right into the clutches of the pursuing savages. There was nothing for it but to head right across the quagmire itself; and so they did.

It soon appeared that both men were experts in this perilous mode of travel. The dexterity with which they leaped from one grass tussock to another wherever there was any support to be had, and the wary skill with which they avoided setting foot on the treacherous spots where there was none, saved them once and again where a less practised 'bog-trotter' would have been instantly swallowed by the fatal slime; and

the advancing rescuers applauded their progress with an encouraging shout.

Meanwhile the savage Wends, seeing their
prey about to escape them, made the air
ring with their wolfish cries, and sent a
shower of arrows after the fliers, while
several of the boldest actually went bound-
ing over the deadly morass in the track
of the runaways, so fiercely bent on their
destruction as to peril their own lives to
achieve it.

But by this time a series of desperate
bounds had brought the fugitives within two
spear-lengths of the causeway along which
Hermann's soldiers were hurrying to their
aid. One moment more and they would
be safe; but just then an unforeseen and
terrible obstacle suddenly stopped them short,
the sight of which was what had wrung
from brave Von der Salza the cry of dismay
that he had just uttered.

Right in front of them yawned a formidably wide gulf of thick black water and half-
liquid mud, into which it was certain death
to fall. Just beyond it lay the causeway
where they would be safe; but such a leap
seemed well-nigh hopeless for weary and
heavily equipped men, and the chasing
savages were now close at their heels, with

yells of ferocious joy like the howl of wolves in sight of their prey.

All at once the foremost runaway was seen to step back a few paces, draw himself together, and shoot out like an arrow into the empty air!

It was a terrible leap, and, as he dashed at it, not a few of the hardy soldiers turned away their faces with a muttered 'God help him!' while through their ranks buzzed a quick, short gasp of terrified excitement. But, to the amazement alike of friend and foe, he flew right over the horrible pit, and alighted safely on the firm causeway beyond.

But the other man, who instantly followed, was not so fortunate. Heavier and less agile than his comrade, he fell short of the leap, and, though he cleared the gulf, failed to make good his footing on the causeway, and was just toppling backward into the fatal pit when his friend seized and dragged him up on to the firm ground.

Then came a shrill, screaming yell—a whiz through the air—a stifled cry—and the rescued man lay bleeding at his comrade's feet, pierced with an arrow!

'Save thyself,' gasped the fallen man, as the other bent over him.

'Not I; it is not my wont to forsake a

comrade in distress,' said the latter, uttering
in those few homely words more real heroism
than many a sounding speech that lives for
ever in history.

That refusal (as he well knew) doomed
him to seemingly certain death; for, though
none of the savages cared to risk the leap
he had taken, those who had followed him
kept shooting at him fiercely across the
slough, while the main body of the Wends
(now reinforced by the stragglers that were
fast coming up) had by this time reached
the entrance of the causeway, and were pressing forward along it to attack him hand to
hand.

Then the brave man laid down his wounded
comrade behind him as gently as a mother,
and, drawing his short broad-bladed sword,
stood grimly at bay.

The grand-master's soldiers (who had set
up a cry of grief and rage as they saw the
hurt man fall) would gladly have flown to
the rescue as fast as their feet could carry
them; but the causeway had been purposely
made so narrow that, in spite of their burning impatience, they were forced to advance
in single file, and the foremost were still
some distance off, when the raging savages
swooped on their prey.

On came the leading Wend with a fierce yell, and, hurling his spear (which the other avoided with a quick bend of his body), dashed in with his hook-shaped axe; but ere he could strike, the stranger's sword flashed and fell, and the savage leader's headless corpse sank with a dull plunge into the hideous quagmire below. The other Wends recoiled for a moment (for, though bred to war from their youth, they had never seen a starker sword-stroke), and then rushed at him once more with brandished weapons and hoarse screams of rage.

Happily they could only attack him one at a time on that narrow way; but a worse peril menaced him from the Wendish archers on the other side of the slough, who hailed on him a storm of arrows. These fell blunted from his steel-cap and stout buff-coat of doubled leather, faced with small lozenge-shaped plates of iron; but his comrade's fate was an ample warning of that which awaited him, if even one of those cruel shafts found an unguarded spot.

But help was now close at hand. There came a lusty shout from behind—a whiz of crossbow bolts striking down three of the Wendish archers—and then, as the fore-most soldiers came dashing up to the spot,

the already daunted savages turned and
fled.

'After them!' shouted Hermann at the
full pitch of his mighty voice; and he and
the bulk of his men went rushing in hot
pursuit of the fliers, while the rest escorted
to the castle the bold champion and his
helpless comrade.

'It is just such men as thou art whom we
need for this work,' said Salza heartily, when,
two hours later, the hero of this daring feat
(having made a good meal, and satisfied
himself that his comrade's wound, though
painful, was not dangerous) entered the hall
where the grand-master and his knights
were at supper. 'As thou say'st that King
Ottocar and his host be nigh at hand to aid
us, truly thou hast well earned the reward
due to him who bringeth good tidings. Fill
thyself a cup of wine, good fellow, and tell
us by what name we may bear in mind so
bold a man-at-arms.'

'No man-at-arms am I, noble sir,' said the
other modestly, with a clumsy salute. 'I am
but a poor shepherd of the Swiss marches'
(borders), 'Hans Bendix by name, vassal to
the lord abbot of Reichenau.'

'A shepherd, say'st thou?' echoed Hermann with a grim smile. 'Nay, then, I

trow *thy* flock will be safe from wolf and
robber. Tell us thy tale, friend, for well I
wot it is worth hearing.'

Hans told him, briefly and modestly, how
the king had wished to send him word to
move against the Wends from one side,
while Ottocar's host pressed them on the
other; how at first every one had hung back
from the seemingly impossible task of finding the way to Marien-Burg through these
pathless forests and perilous swamps, and
getting safe through swarms of blood-thirsty
savages with no knowledge of their tongue;
how he, being familiar with the country and
its language from a former visit to it in
attendance on his master the abbot, had
volunteered for the attempt; and how he
and his comrade (no other than Andrer-
Knecht, the ex-bandit enlisted by Rudolf),
travelling by night and hiding by day, had
all but reached the fort, when they were
detected and pursued by the savages from
whom Hermann had saved them.

'Well and manfully hast thou done!' cried
Salza approvingly, 'and, as our proverb hath
it, deed merits meed. But tell me, good
Hans, sawest thou aught, amid yon heathen
scum that beset thee, of a one-eyed man of
great stature, gaunt as a wolf, with a mighty

ill-favoured visage, and hair red and shaggy as a lion?'

'None such saw I, noble sir,' said Hans, looking interested. 'May I make bold to ask who he is?'

'Marry, when thou hast been a few days with us thou wilt have no need to ask who is the One-eyed Priest, for his very name is a terror to all honest Christian folk from here to the Baltic. This much can I tell thee, that he is the rankest rogue, and the worst fire-brand to kindle these Wendish thieves against us, and the stubbornest servant of Satan who liveth this day 'twixt Vistula and Niemen; and if ever thou art like to fall into his hands, fight to the death rather, for his lightest mercy will be to roast thee alive before the foul idol that he serveth. Well, if he be not here, the better for us all; but hadst thou brought us *his* head, thou hadst done us better service than the slaying of a hundred of the heathen dogs who fell to-day.'

He paused a moment, and then went on in a lighter tone: 'Saidst thou not, good fellow, that thou art of the king's own following? How camest thou by such promotion, being, as thou tellest us, but an unknown shepherd?'

Hans replied by telling, as shortly and simply as he could, the tale of the king's three questions, and his own answers to them. As he ended, the hall rang with a roar of laughter, in which the grand-master himself joined with a will; but as it died away, came floating up to them through the open windows a strange, shrill, high-pitched voice, singing to a fantastic tune words that may be thus translated:

'The Geese were gathered to choose a king;
  "Be the Fox our king," they said,
For he telleth his beads, and wears pilgrim-weeds,
  Looking simple and meek as a maid.
But scarce was he crowned, when he bit the neck
  Of the fattest goose in two.
"Help, help!" screeched the goose. Quoth King
    Fox, "'Tis no use,
  I take but my royal due!"'

Bendix stood amazed (as he well might) to hear this rollicking ditty outside the castle at that hour, in a region where it was all but certain death to be abroad after dark. But Hermann and his knights plainly recognised both song and singer; and Sir Sigismund von Altenburg, the second in command, called out gleefully: 'As I live, it is "Mad Matthew" again!'

CHAPTER VII.

A NIGHTMARE RIDE.

'WHAT HO! Who waits without?' cried the grand-master.

In came two of his guards, to whom he gave orders to throw open the gate, lower the drawbridge, and admit their unlooked-for guest.

'And as for this good fellow,' he went on, pointing to Bendix, 'take him below, and bid my knaves' (*Knaben*, or 'lads') 'treat him like their son.'

'Nay, not so, your worship,' said Hans, with a grin; 'for then must each one give me a sound beating, which I would fain avoid.'

And, with this parting jest (which the manners of the time fully bore out), the ex-shepherd followed his escort out of the hall.

'Who is this Matthew whom ye welcome so?' asked he of one of the guards.

The other told him, readily enough (for Hans had already made friends with half the garrison), that Mad Matthew was a half-

witted hanger-on of the Teutonic Brotherhood, serving them in all sorts of ways, and
flitting ceaselessly from one to another of
their forts. Who he was, or whence he
came, no one had ever found out; but as a
scout he was worth a score of ordinary men,
from his marvellous agility and strength,
coupled with a madman's proverbial cun-
ning. In threading these trackless woods
and perilous morasses without a guide, he
had no match in the whole country; and
his timely warnings had again and again
enabled the knights to foil a sudden attack
of their Wendish foes, whose unceasing
efforts to kill or capture him were all in
vain, though he attacked them wherever he
met them, and even ventured into their
camps as boldly as if he had a charmed life.

'In truth, he knows no fear,' ended the
stout pikeman approvingly, 'and is as prompt
to run into peril as other men to run out of
it. Fire or frost, wolf or bear, swamp-fever
or Wendish spear and arrow, he heeds them
no more than drops of rain! Also the
heathen dogs fear him right sore, for the
more part deem him no man, but a spirit,
saying that no mortal could venture thus
among them and escape unharmed; and
even they who think not so, fear to lay

hand on a madman, as is ever the wont of
these barbarous folk. But here he comes.'

As he spoke, Mad Matthew's spectral form
stalked out of the deep black shadow of the
gateway amid shouts of noisy welcome from
the soldiers (with whom he seemed a prime
favourite); and Bendix, by the light of the
pine-torches that they carried, looked, with a
keen and very natural interest, at the hero
of so many startling feats.

In fact, he was well worth looking at.
Tall as he was, he seemed even taller from
the extreme spareness of his sinewy frame,
gaunt as a wolf, but betraying in its elastic
vigour a strength and agility worthy of his
renown. His dress was as primitive as that
of his Wendish foes; a bear-skin cloak and
cap (from beneath which his long black hair
escaped in twisted elf-locks), wolf-skin leg-
gings and sandals, and an otter-skin belt.

With all this Robinson-Crusoe 'get-up,'
however, there was nothing fierce or warlike
in his face and bearing; on the contrary, his
weather-beaten visage wore a look of frank
and almost boyish good-humour.

What chiefly surprised Bendix was to see
that, in a region where every man carried his
life in his hand, this strange being was wholly
unarmed. But he was still more amazed

when the madman ran up to him, and, seizing him by both hands in a grasp that made even Hans's strong joints tingle, cried out, 'Welcome, brother! thou and I will have work to do together ere long.'

Ere the startled Hans could reply to this strange greeting, Mad Matthew was already on his way up the stair to the great hall. The first thing he did on entering it (to the blank dismay of the men-at-arms who led him in) was to set up a shrill, impish imitation of the crowing of a cock, and then to dance round and round for some time, snapping his fingers like castanets, and making a series of grimaces that sorely tried the gravity of the grand-master himself.

But Hermann and his knights were too well used to their strange follower's queer ways to be at all put out by them; and they knew the hopelessness of finding fault with a man who would have slapped a king on the back, or shaken hands with an emperor on his throne. So they waited quietly to hear what he had to tell them; and they did not wait in vain.

'Guess, cousin Hermann, what manner of steed hath brought me hither,' said he at last, as he made an end of his capers.

'I cannot divine, good Sir Matthew, but I

doubt not thy charger was worthy of so great a warrior,' said Von der Salza, who had long since found that nothing pleased this poor fellow's crazy fancy like treating him as a man of importance, which, in one sense, he certainly was.

'No, I trow thou canst not divine, nor any one else for thee,' chuckled the madman, with a grin which showed that he was keeping in reserve something specially good. 'But thou sayest well that my steed was worthy of me; it was so, in very deed.'

Here he suddenly broke into a laugh so loud and hearty that all the knights, and even the grand-master himself, joined in it without knowing what they were laughing at.

'Well, ye shall hear the tale,' said Matthew; 'but first I must seat myself, for it will not be told in a moment.'

So saying, he curled himself up like a dog on one of the two broad stone ledges flanking the vast fireplace, in which (though it was now the end of April) a huge log-fire still combated the chronic damp of this amphibious region. Then, fixing his keen, restless, glittering eyes on the attentive faces of his hearers, he said, slowly and impressively, 'I have seen the One-eyed Priest!'

At this sudden mention of their most

dreaded foe there was a general start, and, to the madman's visible satisfaction, all heads were at once bent eagerly toward him.

'I—have—seen—him—this—very—night,' he went on, letting fall his words as slowly as if they were precious stones. 'Marry, I am sore athirst; my words will scarce come forth.'

Sigismund von Altenburg, taking the hint, filled him a flagon, which the other emptied at a draught; and then, as if thrilled with new life by the refreshment, he plunged at once into the midst of his story.

'Men tell of a certain gloomy dell in these woods, where the heathen-folk are wont to slay their captives in sacrifice to some foul idol; and it is said that no man may find the place but by losing his way, and that he who cometh thither, cometh to his own death.

'Now there befell me this day a hap that befalleth right seldom, for I lost my way in the forest; and the more I sought it, the more I found it not. But all at once the trees seemed to fall away before me, and forth I came into an open space some twenty paces across, in the midst whereof I beheld dimly a mound of earth, on the which stood a strange and monstrous image. Then understood I that the old rede' (saying) 'was true, and that I, being lost, had found the heathen place of sacrifice and its idol; and of this was I doubly assured when I saw in a ring around the image twelve stumps of felled trees, such as these heathen dogs are wont to call "the circles of the gods."

'At the first I was minded to break in pieces the heathenish image—no hard matter, in sooth, for it was but a wooden block, shaped into some such rude likeness of man as a child might have wrought with a blunt hatchet; and if he were in very deed a god, it must needs have been by virtue of his being uglier than any of his worshippers. But suddenly I heard steps and voices drawing nigh; and it seemed to me best to draw back into the thicket, and wait to see what would befall. Scarce had I done so when there came past, so close that I could well-nigh have touched them, some half-score of the Wendish heathen, armed with spear and axe; and I heard one of them say as he went by: "It is now time to kindle the fire before the altar of our god."

'"That shall be my charge," said another; "and do ye, meanwhile, call Adinglas, and bid him bring hither the victim for the sacrifice."

'Then my heart gave a bound, I warrant
ye; for in Wendish speech Adinglas meaneth
"one-eye," and I judged that he of whom
they spake was none other than the one-
eyed priest, whose death, could I but slay
him, would free all Christian folk of these
parts from their cruellest foe. But how to
get within arm's length of him unseen?

'All at once I bethought me of a rare
sport——'

Here the speaker broke down into a shrill,
screaming laugh, which awoke an echo in
every corner of the old hall. His hearers
eyed him wonderingly, but no one ventured
to speak, knowing that Matthew detested
interruption, and that, if they put him out
in his story, they would never hear another
word of it.

'I had seen,' went on the madman, 'that
these stumps were about the size and height
of a man on his knees, and that three or
four were almost overgrown with weeds and
briars; so I concluded to pull the bear-skin
hood over my face, cover myself with an
armful of brushwood, and pass for a tree-
stump.

'I did it unseen, for he who had charge to
kindle the fire was seeking dead wood in the
thickets, and the rest were gone to summon

their priest. Yet was I none too speedy, for even as I took root, back came my faggot-bearer with his fuel, and in a trice the fire was lit, and blazed up merrily. All at once I saw the Wend start and rub his eyes, and look round the circle once and again; and then he cried out as one amazed: "How now? In place of twelve stumps, lo! there are thirteen!"

'My heart stood still at that, as ye may think; for I wist not they had marked the number so closely. But just then back came the others, with the one-eyed priest in their midst, leading a lame, half-starved horse that had doubtless belonged to some murdered captive. A sorry beast it was, as eye could see; and were I a heathen god, I would break my worshippers' pates if they brought me so scurvy an offering.

'"A wonder, brothers, a wonder!" cried he who had lit the fire. "Here be thirteen stumps in the ring, in place of twelve!"

'"Thou art mad," said one of his comrades; "we have counted them oft."

'"Count them again, and see," quoth he; and when they did so, in very deed they found thirteen; and at that they were sore amazed, and wist not what to do.

'"This is witchcraft," said one, "or

some magic of the Christians.   What shall
we do?"

'"Fools!" screeched the One-eyed Priest,
"think ye any magic can prevail against the
God?   Lo! I will smite all these stumps
with the sacrificial axe that is sacred to him,
and your own eyes shall see the magic give
way!"

'Judge ye if I felt blithe at that word;
but I had no mind to tarry till he should
try if my pate or his axe were the harder,
and as he smote the nearest stump (which
was the next to me) I sprang up with a
scream that might have waked the dead,
hurled my brushwood screen in their faces,
and smote down one man with my spear
and another with my wood-knife!

'I have seen swift runners in my day,
but never saw I mortal man run like yon
heathens.   They were gone ere one could
draw breath, and after them clattered the
freed horse, frightened itself, and affrighting
them yet more.   Only the one-eyed priest
stood his ground, being too sore amazed to
stir hand or foot.   Ere he could move, I
tore down the idol and cast it into the fire,
where his godship blazed and crackled right
merrily; and as the priest sprang to save it,
I leaped on his back with a yell to which

the clamour of a pack of hungry wolves was as nothing!

'Deeming himself in the clutch of a demon, away flew Master One-eye helter-skelter, through swamp and stream and thicket; but I clung to his neck and dug my knees into his ribs, and ever as he yelled, I yelled in answer, till we woke up the whole forest around us. The night-birds rose screaming from the dark trees, and the wolves whined and scattered as we came, and a great wild-boar, grunting and snorting, brake from the thickets right athwart our path, and vanished into the gloom beyond! Never had I such a ride since the day I was born; and thou seest, gossip Hermann, that I said truly that no man might guess what manner of steed brought me hither.

'All at once we burst forth on to open ground, and I beheld the glimmer of the river on our right, and, far in front, the lights of this castle. But just then the One-eye (being well-nigh spent with his race) stumbled and fell, flinging me heavily to the earth, so that I lay awhile as one dazed. But as I lay, methought I heard a splash, as if the heathen had fallen or leaped into the river; and when I arose again, he was nowhere to be espied.

'Then my conscience pricked me that I had not slain him; but seeing that my weapons had been left behind with the dead on the place of sacrifice, what could I do? Perchance it may have pleased heaven to drown him in the river; and, in any case, I have taught these heathen rogues how little their false god availeth to protect them or himself. Gentles, my tale is ended.'

CHAPTER VIII.

CHARGED BY A WILD BULL.

'WELL, cousin Conrad, how lik'st thou our new crusade, thus far?'

'In sooth, cousin Rudolf, it pleaseth me right well. Here be no deserts like the Syrian wastes, and no pestilence to sweep away men like flies; and much I doubt me if the folk in Holy Land can find game enow to furnish forth such a day's sport as we are like to have this morn!'

So spoke, on a fine May morning in east Prussia, Sir Rudolf of Hapsburg and Sir Conrad of Hohenzollern.

Two weeks had passed since Mad Matthew's famous ride, and much had happened in that time. King Ottocar had come at last, with his thousands at his back; and the great plain in front of Marien-Burg, lately so silent and lonely, was now alive with the noise and bustle of a vast camp, the tents of which whitened the dull grey level as far as the eye could reach.

The king had expected a stout resistance, and the grand-master had been prompt to muster his men, as ordered, to aid him in

77

overcoming it. But they found their work much easier than they expected; for though a few scattered bands of savages were met and destroyed, the bulk of the Wends seemed to have fled before the invaders, and every native village that the latter entered was found quite deserted.

At first Ottocar and Von der Salza took this to be only a trick of the enemy, to throw them off their guard before making a sudden attack. But the real fact was widely different, as they learned later on from a captured Wend, whom they examined through their interpreters.

This man told them that the local tribesmen, while preparing for war, had been terrified from their purpose by a strange and fearful portent. The image of their local deity, Radegast the sun-god, had been overthrown and destroyed by an evil spirit that had started up through the earth in the very midst of those who were preparing the sacrifice; and then this image-breaking demon had struck dead two of their best warriors, and had ended by leaping on the back of the high-priest himself, riding him to utter exhaustion through swamp and thicket, and at last flinging him into the river, whence he was saved, barely in time,

by some passing hunters. He had been
sore sick ever since; and the Wends (who
had no mind to face Ottocar's host after
so fearful an omen of evil) had fled northward in a body, carrying their helpless
priest with them.

During the tale, Salza was more than
once seen to smile knowingly; and as
soon as the prisoner had been lead away,
the grand-master laughed aloud. 'Mad
Matthew hath done us good service once
more,' he cried, 'and, mad as they call him,
he hath shown himself shrewder than many
a one who is sound of wits.' Then he
poured into the ears of the wondering king
(who was as much amused as himself) the
whole story of Matthew's exploit in the
circle of sacrifice, and his nightmare ride on
the back of the idol's priest. 'As I am
crowned king,' cried the great Bohemian,
still laughing, 'this Matthew of thine must
be a man of worth. Let some one be sent
quickly to bring him to our presence.'

'He who can do that must be cleverer
than I,' said Hermann bluntly. 'As soon
may one track the wind that bloweth, as
follow Mad Matthew when his mood is on
him. Seven nights agone he left us, since
which time nought hath been seen of him;

and he will not be found, I trow, till such is his own good pleasure.'

'Let be, then,' said Ottocar; 'when he *is* found, he shall not lack his reward. And now, Sir Grand Master, since there be no heathen folk at hand to keep our blades from rusting, we will prove our steel on the wild beasts of these woods, which will doubtless show us good sport.' And he lost no time in getting up a great hunt, which, next to a great fight, was the most popular amusement of all gentlemen in the Middle Ages, who could not be happy unless they were killing something.

In fact this gathering, at which the young knights of Hapsburg and Hohen-zollern were then assisting, was really a 'meet' of the thirteenth century; and these hounds that were leaping and barking around them were trained to hunt not foxes, but wild-boars, stags, wolves, and the terrible 'aur-ochsen' or maned bulls of the northern forests.

The two cousins had not long to wait. All at once the shrill blast of the king's own bugle gave the expected signal; the dogs replied with a joyous bark as they were let loose; the 'prickers' (or, as we should now call them, beaters) pressed

forward, scattering as they advanced; King
Ottocar and his train swept after them, and
the royal hunt began in earnest.

For all the hunters to keep together
amid that pathless maze of swamp and
thicket would have been out of the
question even had they wished it; but the
king himself had given them special orders
to scatter as widely as possible, in order
to bag a greater quantity of game. Thus
he found himself, by the time the sun was
high, almost alone in the forest, his only
companions being Grand Master Hermann
and Rudolf of Hapsburg.

Ottocar was in high good humour, having
overtaken and speared a huge wild-boar
single-handed; and, bent on winning new
trophies, he had left his horse with his
attendants, and was pressing forward on
foot into the deeper woods beyond. Vainly
did the experienced grand-master (who fore-
saw but too well what fatal results might
follow such rashness) try to dissuade him;
the king was deaf to all warnings, and
brave Hermann could only share the perils
that he was powerless to avert.

Rudolf followed as a matter of course,
this being, in fact, his appointed duty, as
he was now attached to the king's person

by the special command of Ottocar himself,
who had taken a great liking to this fearless,
modest, frank young fellow, so hardly used
by fortune, and bearing it so bravely. But,
with this plunge into the wood, Ottocar's
luck seemed to have forsaken him; for
though he could hear, by the distant clamour
of dogs and men, that the hunt was going
on briskly on either side, he and his companions, look as they might, could see no
sign of any game.

'Methinks the beasts as well as the men
have fled this country at our coming!' cried
the king angrily, 'for neither hoof nor hair
can I see of game that is worth hunting.
Wolves there be in plenty, I trow; but who
would blunt steel on such slinking brutes,
whose flesh is carrion and whose very hides
are nought? Could I but meet one of
these wild bulls whereof men talk so much!'

Never was a wish more instantly and
fatally granted. His last words were
drowned by a hoarse bellowing roar, and
up started with a mighty crash out of the
tangled bushes, barely two spear-lengths
from the small clearing in which stood the
king and his comrades, a vast horned head
and black shaggy mane, from which two
fiery eyes glared savagely at the intruders!

Of all the wild beasts which then swarmed over the great forests of Central Europe none was more terrible than the aur-ochs, now practically extinct, but then as formidably supreme in the northern woods as the wild elephant now is in the jungles of India. To the resistless strength and untamable ferocity of his American cousin this European bison added a size fully bearing out even the startling measurements of good old Paul Warnefrid, who had 'seen with his own eyes' (as he tells us) 'skins of aur-ochsen whereon fifteen men might with ease lie side by side.'

For a moment the grim beast—evidently just roused from a nap in one of the 'mud-wallows' that abounded there—stood staring blankly at the three men, with a glow of dull anger in its blinking eyes. Then, all at once, its heavy brain seemed to take in the situation; and, with another savage bellow, it came crashing through the thicket right upon them, snapping stout branches like glass, and tearing away tough creepers like paper.

Brave Von der Salza, who was foremost of the three, sprang nimbly aside from the monster's charge, dealing it a vigorous spear-thrust as he did so. But so mighty

was its rush, that though the bison only
brushed him with its huge shoulder in
thundering past, the shock hurled him to
the earth like a stone from a sling. The
spear went home, however, and remained
fixed in the shaggy flank; but this wound
only enraged instead of checking the savage
brute, which dashed with lowered head
right at the king himself! Ottocar, who
was as brave a man as ever lived, did not
lose his head for a moment even in that
deadly peril. His aim was to do as Salza
had done—to spring aside from the monster's
rush, and stab it as it flew past; but, just
at the critical moment, his foot slipped,
and he fell right in the path of that living
thunderbolt of brute force and fury!

One instant more and the king's hunt
and life would have ended together; the
whole future of Bohemia would have been
changed, and perhaps that of all Europe
as well. But just as all seemed over, came
a sudden and startling interruption.

Rudolf of Hapsburg (who would have
been no true Swiss had he not already
learned to deal with the terrible mountain
bulls from which the Canton of Uri takes
its name) had suddenly brought into play
a device taught him by a veteran Alpine

hunter of that district, whose grandson was one day to be heard of under the name of William Tell. Throwing himself between the king and this charging mountain, the young hero dropped cleverly to the ground, and as the huge mass shot over him, slashed upward at its leg with his short sword, with all the might of his sinewy arm.

There was a hoarse roar of pain, a heavy fall, and then a lusty shout of triumph. Ottocar, springing to his feet as the bull stumbled on its wounded limb and fell, had come to the rescue in turn, and, with one home-driven stab, laid the mighty beast dead ere it could rise.

'Thanks be to God that your Majesty is safe!' said Rudolf fervently, as he eyed the slain monster's vast bulk and terrible horns.

'Thanks be to thee too,' cried the king heartily, 'for though I have many brave men in my train, few there be who would have dared to do what thou hast done.'

Could those two brave men, as their hands met in a hearty brotherly clasp, have foreseen with what terrible irony the far-off future was to undo that day's work, it would have sorely startled them both. But it is not given to man to read the future; and well for him is it, indeed, that he cannot.

CHAPTER IX.

IN THE JAWS OF DEATH.

WHILE Rudolf was thus employed his Hohenzollern cousin was face to face with an adventure even more romantic and perilous.

In obedience to Ottocar's orders, he and the other young knights of the king's train had spread themselves out widely to right and left; and so it came about that Sir Conrad (who had wisely decided to hunt on foot in such a region) found himself picking his way, quite alone, over a narrow strip of firm ground between the edge of the forest and the great morass that protected the approach to Marien-Burg, the tall square tower of which was dimly visible in the distance.

Up to that time he had had no sport whatever; and he was just beginning to feel rather disturbed at the thought of coming in empty-handed at the end of the day, and being laughed at by his more fortunate comrades, when, all at once, he

caught sight of a line of dark objects at
some distance on his left, gliding in and
out of the thick clumps of huge reeds and
long rank grass that masked the fathomless
slime below, with a slinking, sliding motion
that told him at once what they were.
'Wolves!' he muttered; 'do they scent
game, I marvel?'

It seemed likely enough, knowing as he
did the wonderful quickness of these four-
footed pirates in detecting, even at a distance,
the presence of their prey; so, with a slight
smile at the thought of being guided to his
game by wolves in place of hunting-dogs,
he headed in the same direction.

But, all of a sudden, he saw through one
of the thinner spots in the dense reed-jungle
which rose higher than his head, that the
wolves had changed their course, and were
coming right toward him. Were they hunting *him*, then?

It was no pleasant idea, brave as he was;
for he knew what wolves can do when the
rage of hunger has overcome their native
cowardice, and there seemed to be nearly a
score of them in all—terrible odds against
one man in that lonely place, with no
weapons but spear and hunting-knife.

But a moment's thought told him that he

could not be their object of attack; for the
beasts could not possibly see him through
that wall of reeds and wild grass, and the
wind (what little there was of it) was blow-
ing *toward* himself from them. What were
they hunting, then?

Just then the mystery received a sudden
and fearful explanation from a wild cry that
came pealing to his ears, uttered evidently
at no great distance by the shrill, strained
voice of one in mortal agony or terror.
The wolves heard it too, and answered with
that infernal chorus of hungry yells which no
man who has once heard it can ever forget.

In a moment the young knight understood
it all. Someone was struggling for life in
this horrible quagmire, and these foul beasts
had been led toward the fatal spot by the
same ghastly instinct that draws the shark
to the sinking ship, and the vulture to the
lost traveller in the desert. High above the
hellish clamour of the pursuing pack rose
Conrad's lusty shout of encouragement in
answer to that despairing cry, as he burst
through the reeds and flew toward the
sound, springing from tussock to tussock
over the abyss of treacherous mire, and
more than once actually using his spear as
a leaping-pole.

All at once he found himself on one of those raised strips of firm earth, narrow and sheer as the top of a wall, that formed a number of natural causeways amid this hideous chaos which was neither land nor water, but a foul and unnatural mixture of both. But hardly had he made good his footing when the wolves (which were scurrying along the same path from the other side) flew at him with bristling hair and open jaws, and the glare of murder in their cruel yellow eyes.

One mighty spear-thrust struck down the huge gaunt brute that led the attack—a second shared the same fate—and then Conrad, rushing on the recoiling beasts (which could only assail him in pairs on that narrow way) dashed two more over the edge into the slough below, where they speedily sank for ever.

Just then came a furious burst of barking from the woods beyond, so near that the cowardly brutes, already scared by the fall of so many of their number, fairly turned tail and slunk away with a sullen growl.

Then a sudden thought occurred to the young man; from the direction taken by the wolves in their advance, it was plain

that he was between them and their prey,
and that it was not far off. He shouted
once more with all his might; and—yes!
there *was* a reply, but so faint as to show
that he who uttered it must be well-nigh
at his last gasp.

Shouting as he ran, the young knight
flew toward the sound, with a reckless haste
which, in a place where death gaped for
him at every step, was nothing short of
heroic. Nor had he far to go; for, as he
tore his way through a thick briar-clump
that barred the path, a startling scene lay
before him.

Out of the slough of foul beer-coloured
water and clinging mire below rose the
head and shoulders of a man, who would
have sunk outright but for a thick tuft of
coarse wiry grass that he was clutching
with the grasp of desperation. But the
young Swabian's keen eye saw at once that
this last support was already yielding, and
just about to give way altogether.

To his great surprise, Conrad (who had
never doubted that the struggler was one
of his own comrades) now saw the latter to
be a Wend! One glance at the stranger's
sallow complexion and thick yellow hair,
his high cheek-bones and heavy bull-dog

jaw, and, above all, his being bare-headed and to all appearance bare-limbed as well, showed him to be one of the very savages whom Conrad had come to fight.

At sight of the young Swabian, the look of eager hope on the Wend's set, rigid face darkened into the blankness of despair. 'Slay me, then, Christian—I am thy foe!' said he sullenly; 'and rather would I fall by a warrior's hand, than die smothered in this hole like a mired calf.'

'A Christian knight slays not unarmed men, and I come to aid thee, not to harm thee,' said Conrad, as he pushed his spear-shaft within the struggler's reach, and knelt on it to keep it firm. 'Grasp this, and hold fast!'

With one desperate snatch the savage seized the stout wood with both hands, just as the grass-tuft to which he had clung so long gave way; and Conrad, planting him-self as firmly as he could, grasped the Wend's wrists, and strove to tug him out.

So terrific was the clutch of that deadly quicksand, that for a moment it was the turn of a hair whether the gallant rescuer might not sink and perish with the man he would have saved. But at last, with a mighty effort (which the Wend aided with what little strength he had left) the knight plucked his unknown enemy from the jaws of death, and lay gasping beside him.

The hardy young warrior, however, soon regained his breath and strength, but the rescued Wend was in a far worse plight; and Conrad, finding him quite benumbed by his long immersion in the cold, clammy mire, hastened to bring out a flask of strong cordial—no needless travelling companion in those days. A few drops of it did wonders for the fainting man, who, with the aid of his rescuer's arm, was soon able to get on his feet once more.

Then came to Conrad of Hohenzollern a strange and ghostly feeling, as if that lonely and desolate land had taken bodily shape in this lonely and desolate man—as if the wild figure before him, gaunt, haggard, miry, unclothed, were the actual spirit of heathen Prussia, incarnating in that form the dark and cruel past which he and his fellow-crusaders had come to sweep away for ever. One moment more, and the grim illusion had vanished; but it often recurred to his mind in after days, with only too good reason.

'How fares it with thee now?' asked he kindly, speaking in the stranger's own

Wendish tongue (of which he had picked
up a smattering from the king's interpreters
on the long march northward) to inspire
him with confidence.

'Knowest thou our speech?' said the
savage with surprise; for till then they had
spoken German, in which the Wend seemed
tolerably fluent.

'But poorly,' said Conrad; 'howbeit, if
one would dwell in any land, one must needs
learn the speech thereof, and I am minded
to abide here some while, if our lord the
king permit. Methinks thou wilt do well
to taste my cordial once more, for, after
being steeped so long in yon benumbing
quagmire, it may well be that thou canst
neither fight nor fly.'

'Fight I cannot, and fly I will not,'
replied the other proudly; 'but if thou art
minded to take me captive, rather slay me
where I stand, for I will not be taken alive.'

'I have told thee,' said the young hero
firmly, 'that no true knight strikes at a
defenceless man. Slay thee I must not, and
bear thee away captive I cannot; wherefore
go in peace, and if thou thinkest thou dost
owe me any kindness for this day's work,
show some mercy to the next Christian
man who is thy prisoner.'

'Were every Christian like thee,' cried
the Wendish warrior, in a tone of honest
and manly admiration, 'I would myself
become one this very day. But the Christians
have come among us to ravage and destroy;
they have burned our homes, and hewn
down our sacred groves, and overthrown
the altars of our gods, and made their
hands red with the blood of our people.
Betwixt them and us there can be no
peace; but it may be that thou shalt yet
learn that a Wend is not ungrateful.'

So saying, he undid from his throat a
rude necklace of bear's claws (a trophy
which, according to Wendish customs, proved
that the wearer had himself slain the monster
single-handed) and held it out to his rescuer.
'Wear this on thy helmet in battle,' said
he; 'it shall profit thee much. And now
farewell, and bethink thee at times of'—
he paused a moment, and then added,
evidently altering the phrase as he did so
—'of him to whom thou hast shown kindness, though he was thy foe.'

And then, cordially grasping the young
man's hand, he flitted away over the swampy
waste like a shadow, while Hohenzollern
stood gazing after him in thoughtful silence.

CHAPTER X.

CONRAD said nothing of this adventure on rejoining his comrades, having no wish to be laughed at as the unskilled hunter who had found no game all day but a stray savage, and had let *him* escape. But, to his great relief, he found that, so far from his being the only one to return empty-handed, most of his fellow-sportsmen had had no better luck than himself. In fact, the chief honours of the chase had fallen to King Ottocar and Rudolf of Hapsburg; and the young Swiss, in spite of his own modest disclaimer, was justly held to be the real hero of the day.

For some time after the great hunt, their life was almost uneventful, there being nothing to do but to await the coming up of the reinforcements that were on their way to join the king, and the completion of the preparations now making for their final advance northward through the heart of the enemy's country.

The labourers hastily summoned for this
purpose from all the surrounding 'burgs'
of the Teutonic Order formed quite an
army of their own. All along the proposed
line of march, hundreds upon hundreds of
men, protected by strong bodies of soldiers,
were felling trees, burning thickets, bridging
streams, and making firm roads through
the treacherous swamps which were then,
and for ages after, the chief peril of that
wild region.

The Wends having been all scared away
by Mad Matthew's last exploit, the work
went briskly on. Nor was there any lack
of strong arms to carry it out, for thousands
of industrious Dutchmen (made homeless
a few years before by the dreadful inun-
dation that had buried nearly a fourth
of Holland beneath the waters of the
Zuyder Zee) were still flocking to the new
colonies planted by the Teutonic Order
in east Prussia, where they were heartily
welcome, and did good service in many
ways.

During this period of enforced inaction,
Rudolf of Hapsburg, true to his rule of
picking up fresh knowledge wherever he
went (though he little dreamed how and
where such knowledge was one day to

profit him) had many a talk with the
grand-master's chaplain, a good old Bene-
dictine monk, from whom he learned all he
could of this strange region and its wild
people.

Nor could he have applied to a better
source for such information ; for good Brother
Marcian was a perfect mine of learning on
Wend-land and all connected with it, and,
when once fairly launched on the full flow
of his stories of that wild land (then far
more unknown and fabulous than Central
Africa now), not only Rudolf, but his
Hohenzollern cousin as well, would gladly
listen to him by the hour.

He told them how, when first visited by
a sharp Greek commercial agent of the
time of Alexander the Great, from the
Greek colony of Massilia (Marseilles) to report on the prospects, if any, of business
on the Baltic coast, Semnonia (as that part
of the Prussian sea-board was then called)
was found to produce nothing but amber
and furs, and to be inhabited by ' certain
Suevi, men great of stature and fierce of
aspect, with stern grey eyes and shaggy
hair,' and about as civilised as the wild
beasts that they hunted.

But when five centuries more had gone

by, the great tide of conquest that was hurling all the races of Northern Europe, wave on wave, against the crumbling Roman Empire, swept into its whirl even these remote Suevic tribes, who, rushing southward like the rest, left their Semnonian hunting‑grounds unpeopled. Then some straggling bands of Slavonian savages, drifting westward from the great plain now called Russia, found and occupied this deserted region, and named it 'Wend‑land' after themselves.

These Wends, said Marcian, brought with them from Asia the rude rites and savage customs of their Scythian ancestors; and his two hearers listened with redoubled interest as he told that the horse-sacrifice to the sun‑god Radegast, so startlingly interrupted by Mad Matthew, had come down direct from the Massagetæ with whom King Cyrus of Persia had fought eighteen centuries before!

'And a learned Greek clerk of old time, Herodotus by name,' added the monk, 'saith the barbarians did thus because they thought it meet to offer "the swiftest of creatures to the swiftest of gods."'

The Wends had for a time had it all their own way in Prussia, and set up,

near the present site of Stettin, the temple
of their three-headed idol, Triglaf; 'tri-galvi'
meaning 'three heads' in Wendish, as it
now does in Russian. But, in 928, the
emperor, Henry the Fowler, took their
chief fortress, Brannibor, now known as
Brandenburg; and, for more than a century
after, the Margraves of Dittmarsch on one
side, and the Polish Dukes of Masovia
(Warsaw) on the other, kept driving them
back and back by sheer dint of hard fighting, confining them at last to the region
in which they now were.

But the great event of Wendish history,
in Marcian's eyes, was the martyrdom, in
997, of St Adalbert, the Bishop of Prag,
who, taking his life in his hands, had
ventured bravely into that savage wilderness in the hope of converting its heathen
people, and had been murdered in the
attempt.

The two young knights looked at each
other with sparkling eyes, but neither
spoke.

'And the idol grove wherein he was
slain,' ended the old monk solemnly,
'which they call "Romova" in their heathen
speech, still standeth in a waste spot compassed about by the sea, far away to the

north; and men say that he who can make
his way into that grove, and cast down
the three-headed idol in the midst thereof,
shall overthrow heathendom in this land,
once and for ever.'

'Ha! hearest thou that, cousin Rudolf?'
cried Hohenzollern, with a deeper flush
on his ' bright young face. 'How if this
adventure were reserved for thee and me
to achieve? With God's help, kinsman, we
will at least try!'

'With God's help, we will!' echoed Hapsburg, with equal energy.

'May He be with ye, my sons, and
bless ye both!' said the monk kindly.
'Assuredly ye shall do great things, and
shall still prevail.'

Early one morning, not long after this,
King Ottocar, as he sat in council with
his courtiers and captains, and received the
reports of the various scouts whom he had
sent forth, heard a great shouting and
tumult from the north side of the camp,
where the Knights of the Teutonic Brotherhood had quartered their soldiers; and the
king, surprised at this sudden uproar, bade
one of his attendants go and see what it
meant.

'Lord king,' said the man, returning, 'he

whom they call " Mad Matthew " has just come into the camp, and they are welcoming him.'

'Aha!' cried the king; 'this falls as I would have it. Long have I wished to see him, and of a surety he beareth tidings worth hearing. Go quickly, and bring him to me.'

But there was no need; for just then the illustrious Matthew himself was seen stalking majestically toward them, at the head of a retinue almost as large as the king's own. The news of his arrival had already run through the camp, and at every step the train of his followers kept growing like a rolling snowball. Amid looks of silent dismay from the courtier-circle, he came right up to the king, and, without doffing his cap or showing any signs of reverence, called out in a loud, familiar tone, 'I salute thee, my brother; the King of the Wilderness greets the King of Bohemia.'

'Welcome, royal brother,' said Ottocar, who, though in his later years fiercely impatient of the lightest jest against himself, seemed rather amused than offended by the madman's free-and-easy behaviour. 'I have wished to meet thee this many a

day; but thou hast no doubt been fully
busied elsewhere.'

'Aye,' cried the other; 'like most kings,
I have always plenty to do; but, very
*un*like most kings, I *do* it!'

The smooth-spoken courtiers stood aghast
at this impudence; but three or four of
the listening soldiers grinned outright, and
the king himself replied only with a good-
humoured smile.

'It is not every king,' pursued the madman complacently, 'who can be, like me,
three men in one. Here stand I to maintain that I am at once a soldier, a hunter,
and a minstrel.'

'A minstrel, say'st thou, brother?' cried
Ottocar, anxious to humour to the utmost
a man who might be of such priceless
service to him. 'Nay, then, thou art
doubly welcome; for though it is not
always that a king rejoiceth to meet
another king, there is no court, I trow,
where a minstrel is not a welcome guest.
Nought better can we wish than a blithe
lay to brighten these grave councils of
ours; for, as the old saying goes, "Pipe
and tabor lighten labour." May we crave a
proof of thy skill?'

'Willingly, my good brother,' said the

self-styled 'King' Matthew, with a con-
descending air that made all the soldiers
grin anew; and, to the secret horror of
all who had heard it before, he struck up,
loud enough to be audible to the whole
assembly, his song of 'The Geese Choosing
a King':

'The Geese were gathered to choose a king;
  "Let the Fox be our king," they said,
For he telleth his beads, and wears pilgrim-weeds,
  Looking simple and meek as a maid.
But scarce was he crowned, when he bit the neck
  Of the fattest goose in two!
"Help, help!" screeched the goose. Quoth King
    Fox, "'Tis no use,
  I but take my royal due!"'

Some of the nobles began to frown, as
well they might; but the king himself
laughed heartily, and bade the singer go
on, which he did without needing any
invitation:

'Then up came the Wolf, and he licked his chops,
  And thus to King Fox said he:
"Lord king, do but give me my share of the geese,
  And I will thy chancellor be!"'

A ripple of half-stifled laughter hailed this
bold hit at the unpopular chancellor, who
eyed the daring jester as if he would have

torn him in pieces; but Matthew, not a whit daunted, went on as briskly as ever:

> 'Then out of the dirt crawled slugs and worms,
>   And the king asked, "Who are you?"
> And the worms said, "To thee we look for food,
>   For we are thy courtiers true!"'

Here the general laughter swelled into a perfect roar, so loud that the singer was fain to cease his edifying ditty, though the mocking grin with which he eyed the enraged courtiers showed that he was not silent from any fear of them.

'And now, brother Ottocar,' said he, as he took his seat without ceremony on a huge stone beside him, 'I have somewhat to tell thee which it concerns thee much to know. Like other kings, thou art ill served, for one of thine own followers hath betrayed thee!'

'Betrayed?' cried Ottocar, in a voice like the roll of distant thunder, as a black frown darkened his noble face. 'When? how? by whom?'

'As to the when,' said the madman, who enjoyed, like all his class, the telling of anything strange and startling, 'it was on the day of thy great hunt. As to the how, a follower of thine had in his hands thy worst enemy, one who is the life and soul of these heathen wolves that war against us, and who came hither with full purpose to slay thee; and that same follower of thine let him go!'

'Why, kinsman, what ails thee?' whispered Rudolf of Hapsburg to his cousin Conrad, startled at the sudden change in the latter's bright, boyish face. 'What hath a charge of treason to do with thee or me? as well might one accuse us of cowardice!'

But Hohenzollern made no reply.

'And who, then, was the traitor that did thus?' asked the king, in a voice half-choked with rising fury, while his dark face glowed like heated iron.

'His name I know not; but I will teach thee how to find him out.'

'Speak!' roared Ottocar, springing to his feet like a roused lion. 'Speak out, and, so help me St Severin, thou shalt see, ere we part, that Ottocar of Bohemia knoweth how to requite both a good turn and an ill one!'

'Hearken, then,' said the other, with stern impressiveness. 'I have been once more among the heathen, and have learned that Prince Radomir, their great champion (nephew to King Mistevoi himself) stole

hither on the day of the hunt, meaning to
slay thee as the chief foe of his people.
But, coming among the quagmires, he lost
his weapons, and was sore bemired withal.
There he was found by a knight of thine,
who slew him not, but let him go free; in
requital of which good service the heathen
gave him a necklace of bear's claws, bidding
him wear it in battle as a charm against all
weapons.   With whomsoever that necklace
is found, the same is he!'

As the tale ended (told by Matthew with
a bitter and scornful emphasis that showed
what he thought of it) there was a clash of
arms as the king's captains clutched sword
and dagger, and glared round as if in quest
of the traitor; and Ottocar himself clenched
his strong hand till the knuckles grew white.

'Let instant search be made——' he was
beginning fiercely, when a clear, firm voice
broke in on his speech.

'It needeth not, lord king; I alone am
guilty, and here do I submit me to thy
good pleasure.'

And Conrad of Hohenzollern, stepping
forth from the crowd, folded his arms on
his breast, and stood firm as the rocks of
his Swabian castle.

A quick gasp of amazement hissed through

the fearful silence that followed; and the
king (his anger lost in astonishment) stared
blankly at the self-doomed culprit, as if
doubting even the evidence of his own
senses. 'Thou ravest, man,' said he im-
patiently. 'Thou a traitor? I would as
soon deem mine own self one!'

The grandees, with the true courtier instinct, had at once shrunk away from a
man who was under the king's displeasure;
but Hapsburg, obeying only the impulse of
his own gallant heart, sprang to his cousin's
side, and sent his voice through the ominous
stillness, clear and unfaltering as ever:

'Thou art right, lord king; and when my
kinsman smote down the Baron of Geierfels
with a broken sword at Rheinfelden, before
thine own eyes, there was no talk of traitors
or treason then. Here stand I, Rudolf of
Hapsburg, ready to meet with sword and
lance any man of my degree who shall dare
to say that my cousin, Conrad of Hohenzollern, is aught but a loyal and honourable
knight.'

Rudolf's slap-dash intervention did more
for his cousin's cause than the most artful
pleading could have done; for the brave
king's manly heart was touched by the
young noble's chivalrous support of one

from whom all else had shrunk away,
and doubly so by the memory of Conrad's
heroic venture of life and limb against the
most formidable swordsman in Rhineland,
in defence of a few obscure strangers.

'What say'st thou, Sir Conrad?' the king
asked, in a perceptibly milder tone. 'It is
said that children and fools speak the truth;
hath this witless man spoken it, or no?'

'He hath spoken that which he thought to
be the truth, and, in so speaking, he hath
done well,' said Conrad, with a glance of
kindly forgiveness at the troubled Matthew,
who, realising for the first time what his
reckless accusation had brought upon one
of the two brave lads whom he loved with
the unreasoning affection of a dog, wore
such a look of piteous surprise as a child
might wear on finding that it had done
grievous mischief where it had meant to be
a help.

'How meanest thou?' asked the king
hastily.

'That I saved a Wend whom I found
perishing in the mire, I freely admit,' said
the young hero, raising his bright face, and
looking fearlessly around him; 'but that I
knew him to be Prince Radomir, or to
purpose murdering thee, I utterly deny; and

may God so deal with me as my denial is true!'

This solemn appeal had a marked effect on all who heard it; for that simple downright age firmly believed that such an attestation, if made by one who was really guilty, must draw down on him the direct and instant vengeance of the Power challenged by his impious perjury.

The frowning nobles unbent their brows, and the king's stern face softened visibly as he said, 'Tell thy tale, young sir; for never will I condemn any man unheard, and thee least of all.'

Briefly and modestly, Hohenzollern did so; and when he ceased to speak, a deep and gloomy silence sank over the whole assembly.

'Hast thou yet the bear-claw chain he gave thee?' asked Ottocar at last.

'I have,' said Conrad, producing the necklace; 'but I wear it not, deeming it not meet for a Christian man to wear a heathen charm.'

'Nay, there thou art over-scrupulous, Sir Conrad,' cried the king. 'No charm seemeth it to me, in sooth, but rather a token whereby he who gave it may know thee in the fight, and try his force with thine, even as brave men are wont to do.'

The young knight's bold blue eyes sparkled, but he made no reply.

'As for thee, good friend,' said Ottocar to the dejected Matthew, 'vex thyself no more. Thou hast done right, as this young knight saith; and if thou hast not unmasked a traitor, it is because there is none such here to unmask. Thou hast done us manful service ere now, and I trow thou wilt yet do more.'

The sudden light that broke over Mad Matthew's downcast face at the last words was a sufficient answer on that point.

'And now to thy matters, Sir Conrad of Hohenzollern,' went on the king. 'Inasmuch as thou hast saved a helpless man from death, thou hast done knightly and well; inasmuch as thou hast let go an enemy and a murderer, thou has done ill, and it behoves thee to make amends. Hearken, then, to my judgment. On the morrow begins the last bout of our wrestle with the heathen, and thou shalt wear Radomir's token in thy helmet, and find him out by it if thou canst. If in one month and one day he be captive or slain, thou art quit of all blame; but if not, thou shalt come back to me wherever I be, and abide my doom, be it what it may.'

CHAPTER XI.

A TRAITOR'S BLOW.

ABOUT a week later, just in the height of that memorable summer (the hottest and driest that had been known in that damp region for many a year), two men were hovering mysteriously on the skirts of one of those dense and pathless woods which, alternating with broad belts of oozy morass, stretched northward right away to the flat, sandy shore of the far-off Baltic.

Wood-cutters these men could not be, for they had no axes; nor could they be hunters, for, so far from pressing on into the depth of the wood, where game was to be found in plenty, they seemed specially careful to keep out of it. Yet, curiously enough, they kept holding up their hands and turning their faces to and fro (as if to make sure from what quarter the wind blew) just as hunters would have done.

But all at once the short, square, red-haired man on the right (who was no other than Andrer-Knecht, Hapsburg's brigand recruit) lifted his head as if listening intently, and then crouched down behind a briar-clump, signing to his comrade, Hans Bendix, to do the same. 'Here come other folk, friend Hans,' he whispered; 'let us bide still till we know who they be, for in these parts every stranger is a foe.'

Presently two horsemen came up at a slow pace, followed by thirty or forty foot-soldiers. 'I hate this Conrad of Hohenzollern to the death,' said one of the riders, a large and powerful man, with a fearful scar on his face; 'and while this mark that he gave me shall last, no fear lest I forget what I owe him.'

'And I, kinsman,' growled the other, whose shaggy red beard hung over his cuirass, 'have just as little love for yon beggarly young upstart, Rudolf of Haps-burg, who hath thrust himself thus into our king's favour; and if ever I have him at my mercy——'

'Here is choice Christian good-will,' muttered Andrer-Knecht with a grim smile, as the voices died away. 'My master, Sir Rudolf, must know of this forthwith; for yon red-beard is Count Valens of Thuringia, who never breaketh his word when he vows to do evil!'

'And the other,' said Hans, 'is the wicked Baron of Geierfels, a greater villain than his kinsman, if greater may be. I deemed he had died when the young knight of Hohenzollern smote him down at Rheinfelden; but he hath had better luck than many a better man. Belike he is but now come up with these new forces of ours, and hath not yet had time for mischief; but, be that as it may, Sir Conrad shall hear of this ere the world be a day older.'

'Right,' said Andrer-Knecht; 'and now, comrade, let us to this gear, for methinks the wind standeth right to aid us in the work.'

They deliberately fired the brushwood in front and on either side, and then drew back to watch the progress of the flames, which (trees and bushes alike being dry as tinder from the long drought) raged so fiercely that all that part of the wood was soon one red and roaring blaze, forcing even the two hardy soldiers to fall back to a distance.

Even while they were still kindling the undergrowth, four or five curls of thickening smoke, creeping upward from various points along the edge of the wood, told that it had been fired in several other places at once, this being the last and deadliest weapon used by the invaders in what King Ottocar had rightly called 'the last bout of their wrestle with the heathen.'

In fact, the king's mode of war was a very simple one, the same by which, four centuries later, the Puritan settlers of New England cut off a whole tribe of hostile Indians. It was simply to fire the woods in which the savages were lurking, and, when the flames drove them out, to fall upon them and kill them all. The result of this strategy is best given in the words of Grand Master Hermann, who shared with Count Valens of Thuringia the command of the troops engaged in clearing that part of the country, while Ottocar, with the main army, was pressing the Wends elsewhere : 'It befell that on the feast of the blessed Baptist, the favour of Heaven sent us an exceeding strong wind, which mightily helped the fire that we had set to the woods wherein these accursed heathens had taken refuge. Being unable to abide the fire, they fled forth to the open plain, where our men, being set there in readiness, did fall upon them with such good heart and courage, that, by God's mercy, we slew there, at one heat, some six hundred of the idolaters ; to His holy name be all the glory !'

While the worthy grand-master was engaged in the pious duties that he described so complacently, the men sent to fire the forest, having done their work, went off to rejoin their respective detachments; and here Bendix and Andrer-Knecht parted, the one going to the right and the other to the left.

Andrer-Knecht had the good luck to fall in, almost at once, with his master Rudolf, whom he hastened to warn of Count Valens's evil designs, to the no small grief and surprise of the gallant young Swiss; for though he had already noted that the fierce Thuringian looked on him with no friendly eye, it was a sore shock to his frank and chivalrous nature to find that, even in the midst of what was then held to be a 'holy war,' this man, whom he had never wronged in any way, could regard him with so deadly a hatred from a motive of mean personal jealousy.

Meanwhile Hans Bendix was less fortunate in his search for Conrad of Hohenzollern, though he little dreamed what fearful consequences and what bitter regrets were to flow from an accident for which he was in no way to blame. He did indeed, by a desperate effort, succeed in catching up a part of the detachment under Conrad's command;

but Conrad himself (to warn whom against Geierfels he had made all this haste) was no longer with it.

In fact, victors and vanquished alike were by this time scattered over the whole face of the country; for, though the Wends had fought like tigers, there could be but one issue to a fight between skin-clad savages armed with reed arrows or brittle spears, and trained soldiers sheathed in steel, who wielded maces, battle-axes, and two-handed swords. In a trice the Wends were flying for their lives, hotly chased by the conquerors.

All through this maddening hurly-burly Conrad kept steadily on the track of one man, in whom he thought he recognised Patkul, a native chief formidable alike for his matchless prowess and pitiless cruelty, whose fall would go far to hasten the end of the war itself.

But, like a true savage, Patkul (for it was he) was ready either to fight when fighting was required, or to run away when running away seemed the wiser course. Through all the wild whirl of flight and pursuit, he held straight on toward the waste of pathless morass beyond, and, with a mocking laugh, darted over the rude bridge of two unsteady pine-trunks which spanned the wide gulf of

half-liquid mire that bordered it, evidently
deeming himself quite safe there.

But he had mistaken his man. Conrad,
still close beside him, flew in turn over the
trembling log-bridge ere his foe had time
to overthrow it, and in a moment was at
his heels again with uplifted sword.

One glance over his shoulder showed the
savage Wend that his assailant was alone,
and this was all he wanted. Quick as
thought, he sprang round with a yell of
ferocious joy, and, whirling up the terrible
club that had already brained two of
Conrad's best soldiers, flew at the brave
young Swabian like a hungry tiger.

All that followed seemed to Conrad like
the confusion of a nightmare. A savage
face glaring into his own—a dim sense of
furious blows given and taken — a dull,
numbing pain as he was beaten down on
his knees by a crushing stroke—a desperate
thrust upward; and then he found himself
leaning dizzily on his elbow and knee, with
his terrible foe lying dead beside him.

But, weak as he was from the strain of
that death-grapple, the infernal yell that
came to his ears at that moment made him
spring to his feet as if suddenly restored
to all his lost strength; and his swimming

eyes saw dimly, not fifty yards away, a
score of armed Wends hurrying toward
him as fast as the broken ground would let
them, with furious gestures and wolfish cries.
They had evidently seen their great champion
fall beneath his sword; and he knew what
mercy Patkul's slayer might expect from
these fierce savages, still smarting under
their defeat of that day.

Conrad turned and ran, as best he might,
toward the log-bridge that led to the open
plain, and was within a few paces of it,
when an armed knight came galloping up to
the farther brink of the slough. Conrad's
heart leaped at this unlooked-for aid; but
it sank again as he knew his mortal foe,
the cruel Baron of Geierfels!

'Welcome, fair sir,' cried the baron jeeringly, as he sprang from his horse, and
eyed, with the grin of a demon on his
scarred face, the man whose sword had disfigured him for life. 'I have long owed
thee a heavy debt, and right glad am I
to be able to pay it at last!'

As he spoke, the ruffian stooped over the
two pine-logs that were Conrad's only way
of escape, seized one in each hand, and,
with a mighty effort, tugged them clear of
the opposite bank, and flung them into the

horrible quagmire below, where they were instantly swallowed up for ever. Then, waving his hand in mocking farewell to the doomed man whose last hope of life he had just destroyed, the villain rode slowly away.

But a fresh burst of yells made him glance over his shoulder as he did so, just in time to see Hohenzollern fall heavily to the earth, and the howling murderers close round him like wolves around a crippled deer.

CHAPTER XII.

THE TONGUE OF THE SERPENT.

WHILE all this was passing on one side of the battle-field, Rudolf of Hapsburg, on the other, had his hands full on his own account. In the heat of the chase most of his men had got scattered, and only a few were left with him when he heard all at once, just in front of him, a burst of triumphant yells, mingled with the faint and failing sound of the German war-cry. It was plain that, in this quarter at least, the savages were getting the best of it, and he lost not a moment in hurrying to the spot.

Just at this point the level plain ended, and before him lay a succession of broad, low, sandy downs (they could not be called hills), from behind the nearest of which this clamour seemed to issue. In a trice Rudolf and his men were on the crest of the slope, and before them lay a startling sight.

In a deep hollow just below, a dozen German men-at-arms were fighting for their lives against at least five times their number

of Wends, who were pressing them on all
sides with savage cries and seemingly resistless fury. The German leader, a tall and
powerful man in gilded armour, stood with
one foot on his dead war-horse, whirling
his two-handed sword round his head, and
shredding off the Wendish spear-points like
bulrushes.

In dealing one of these sweeping strokes,
he happened to turn his face full toward
Rudolf, just as the latter crowned the
ridge; and Hapsburg knew at a glance the
harsh features and shaggy red beard of the
very man against whose ill-will he had just
been warned—Count Valens of Thuringia!

'Hapsburg to the rescue!' shouted the
brave young Swiss, in a voice like a trumpet-
blast; and down he charged into the thick
of the fray.

At that instant Valens sank to the earth
beneath a crushing blow.

One moment more and all would have
been over with the savage Thuringian, and
Rudolf's worst foe swept from his path
for ever. But Hapsburg struck down the
assailant in turn, and, bestriding the prostrate count, hewed right and left at the
whirl of fierce faces that eddied around him
like the phantoms of a nightmare.

Then, for a few seconds, all was one mad welter of hand-to-hand fight, blows falling like hail, and death coming blindly, no one knew whence or how. Twice over, Andrer-Knecht's quick eye and strong arm saved his young lord from a stroke that would have ended him there and then; but all at once Rudolf saw the ex-robber beaten down in turn, and sprang in just in time to catch on his shield the assailant's second blow.

'Radomir! Radomir!' yelled the Wends, rushing up to the spot.

'Hapsburg! Hapsburg!' shouted Rudolf's men-at-arms in reply, bearing them back with a furious charge.

Back came to Rudolf's mind, with a sudden flash, Conrad's mention of this Radomir as the greatest of Wendish warriors.

'Art thou Radomir?' quickly asked the young knight of his opponent.

'I am he, and thy foe,' said the other proudly; and to it they went.

Though one of the best knights of his time, our hero had fairly met his match for once. All his blows were wasted on the empty air by the lightning-swift movements of his foe's gaunt, sinewy frame; and he was more than once sent reeling back by such a stroke as he had never felt till then. At last, with a dexterous slash, he cut the Wend's axe-shaft in two; and Radomir, flinging the useless weapon fiercely away, sprang upon the young Swiss, and grappled him with a clutch of iron. Rudolf, in turn, fastened on him like a wild-cat, hoping to end the war at one blow by its great leader's fall; and the two rolled on the ground together.

But just then a ringing trumpet-blast, mingling with the thunder of charging hoofs, told that the king himself was at hand; and Radomir, slipping from Rudolf's clutch like a ghost, vanished with all his remaining men over the ridge, just as Ottocar and his knights came pouring into the fatal hollow.

To Hapsburg's great relief, Andrer-Knecht proved to be but slightly hurt, 'being armed in a skull of proof,' as he said with a grin. At the same moment Count Valens was seen to rise slowly, stunned but unwounded; and, coming up to Rudolf, he growled out a few words of ungracious thanks, which his scowling face amply belied. But Andrer-Knecht's cynical comment showed that he, like his master, took this ruffian's gratitude for what it was worth. 'He is now doubly

thy foe, my lord,' said he, with a meaning
look after the count, 'for even could he
pardon an offence, he can never forgive
a benefit.'

The sun, now beginning to sink, was
darkened even before its setting by the vast
cloud of thick black smoke that billowed up
from the burning forest. The king gave
orders to sound the 'recall'; and, at the
well-known signal, all the scattered detachments within hearing came straggling in.

Rudolf's keen eye caught the flutter of
the Hohenzollern banner, and he hurried
toward it to greet his cousin, of whom he
had seen nothing all day. But his heart
died within him as he saw in the midst of
the troop, not his kinsman's bright young
face, but a riderless war-house, led by a
man-at-arms. 'Where is your master?'
asked he hastily.

'We know not, my lord,' said the banner-
man gloomily. 'We found his war-steed
running loose over the plain; but of himself
we have seen nought.'

Hapsburg looked keenly at the horse, and
was greatly relieved to see no sign of blood
on it. But this, after all, proved nothing;
for, if Conrad had followed the pursuit into
the morass, he would have had to leave his

horse and go on foot; and Rudolf's brighten-
ing face darkened again as he recalled the
deadly ambush into which Count Valens had
fallen, and thought how easily a similar
snare might have entrapped his daring kinsman.

'What! Is Sir Conrad of Hohenzollern
missing?' said the king, as, seated on his
war-horse, he watched the stragglers come
in. 'Much would it grieve me if aught of
ill had befallen him. Who hath seen him
this day?'

For a moment no one replied; but Rudolf
suddenly saw an infernal smile light up the
scarred face of Geierfels, to whom a new
and frightful scheme of vengeance on the
man who had defeated and disfigured him
had just suggested itself.

'Sorely am I grieved to say it,' said the
baron at last, with a great show of unwill-
ingness; 'but since thou askest, lord king,
the truth must be told. I have seen Sir
Conrad, and he has gone over to the
enemy!'

In fact, this double-dyed villain, whose
quenchless hatred reached even beyond the
grave, had determined (fearing no contradiction, now that death had sealed his victim's
lips) to blast the good name of the man

whom he had himself sent to destruction,
and to brand his memory with the undying
shame of a traitor.   His cruel words were
followed by a stupefied silence, which was
suddenly and startlingly broken.

'Liar!' shouted Rudolf of Hapsburg in a
voice of thunder, as he strode forward and
confronted with flaming eyes the slanderer
of his lost kinsman; 'dares thy serpent
tongue drop venom on him, when dead,
whom thou wouldst have feared to face
when living?   Methinks yon trench in thy
face might have taught thee courtesy, could
such a beast ever learn it!'

At this plain speaking (which, after all,
was only a fair average sample of the
language used by gentlemen in that age)
the baron's brutal face wore a look worthy of
the ugliest demon in St Anthony's Tempta-
tion.   Too choked with rage to speak, he
drew his sword; and at once Rudolf's blade
flashed out likewise.

'Be still, on your lives!' roared the king,
laying *his* hand on his sword as if he meant
to keep the peace by knocking both dis-
putants on the head at once.   'What!
brawl ye in our presence as in a wayside
tavern?   Sir Rudolf of Hapsburg, how hast
thou dared——'

'Lord king,' said Rudolf firmly, 'I am thy true and loyal subject in all matters wherein I owe thee obedience; but none the less am I a free noble of the empire, who dares to speak the truth in the presence of any man living, were it our holy father the Pope. In thy presence, then, I tell my cousin's slanderer that he lies; and I will maintain it in fair field, with sword and with lance, unless he be coward as well as felon and traitor!'

By this time the whole throng was in an uproar, some siding with Rudolf and some with Geierfels; and, in that fierce age, when every man was prompt to enforce his opinion with hand and sword, such a dissension might easily have ended in a general battle. But King Ottocar, with the dignity that he seldom lost, waved back the excited crowd, and, rising in his stirrups, called out in a clear, commanding tone, which rose high above all the din: 'Peace, sirs! it must not be said that Christian men ended a day of holy war against the heathen by falling foul of each other. This matter must be fully heard on both sides, and on the morrow we will ourselves look into it as is meet. Meanwhile keep the peace, and be assured that justice shall be done.'

CHAPTER XIII.

FALSE WITNESS.

ON the next day the king made good his
promise of a full investigation of this
strange case; and, by good luck, he was able
to do so without interfering with the progress of the campaign. The whole army had
been compelled to halt at this point, by the
necessity of giving the forest-fires time to
burn out, and of sending on working parties
to bridge over the perilous sloughs in front
of them. These gangs were protected by
strong bodies of soldiers; but they were
hardly needed. The Wends seemed fairly
cowed by the fearful reverse of the previous
day, for no sign of a foe was to be seen.

Ere the sun was high, the camp-equipage
that followed the army had come up, the
king's tent was pitched, and his heralds were
summoning, by sound of trumpet, all his
nobles and knights to a special council;
and with the rest came the two challengers,
each escorted by a small party of chosen
friends.

Geierfels was sullen and scowling, with a gleam of concentrated malice in his small, deep-set, cruel eyes. Hapsburg was all aglow with generous enthusiasm, and looked so gallant and so manly that even those who loved him least were fain to own that any cause might well be proud of such a champion.

But, little as one might have expected it, the savage baron had many supporters among the assembled nobles. Some took his side from admiration of his warlike renown, some from a mere instinctive tendency to side with an old acquaintance against a stranger, and not a few (to their eternal shame) from a mean personal spite at the two cousins, arising partly from a jealousy of the fame already acquired by such young knights, and partly from a secret envy of their evident favour with the king.

Conspicuous amid the baron's friends appeared the brawny bulk and thick red beard of Count Valens, who, as he passed Rudolf, darted a glance at him which the shrewd young Swiss was at no loss to interpret.

All looked expectantly for the wild figure of Mad Matthew, never doubting that he would be present at a scene so congenial to his restless and excitable nature; and many of the cousins' well-wishers hoped secretly that the madman might be able to contradict the baron's charge by his own personal testimony, which, unreliable as it would be now, carried weight in an age which believed that one whom Heaven had deprived of reason was compensated with the gift of superhuman knowledge in other ways. But these hopes were vain, for, look as they might, Matthew was nowhere to be seen.

All being now ready, the heralds proclaimed silence, and the king, from his seat in the midst, spoke with slow and solemn emphasis:

'Nobles, knights, and gentlemen all! We be gathered this day, as ye wot well, to make inquiry into a charge of treason and desertion against Sir Conrad of Hohenzollern; the said charge being made by the noble Baron Otto of Geierfels, here present, and denied by Sir Conrad's kinsman, the good knight Sir Rudolf of Hapsburg, here present also. Now, forasmuch as Sir Conrad himself is not in presence to plead his own cause, it much behoveth us, as crowned king and Christian man, to see that he hath full and fair justice, and pray to God that He may enlighten us so to do.'

He paused, and for a moment or two no sound broke the gloomy silence, during which the lookers-on exchanged meaning glances.

'Sir Otto of Geierfels,' resumed the king, 'thou art the accuser in this case. Stand forth, then, and tell plainly all thou know'st of the matter.'

Forward stalked the baron, his bulky form and brutal visage making a startling contrast to the slim, well-knit frame and bright, expressive face of Hapsburg, who stood eyeing him with a look of calm disdain.

'Lord king,' said Geierfels, in a voice like the growl of a bear, 'I followed yester-even with the rest, till, in the heat of pursuit, my men were scattered from me, and I was left alone. But I held straight on after a certain Wend who seemed to be a chief, being minded that he should not escape, both because he was a man of great prowess in the fight, and also that me-thought I had heard one call him Patkul!'

At that dreaded name there was a visible stir in the crowd, and the king himself bent eagerly forward to listen.

'Ere I could overtake him,' the baron went on, 'the heathen, being exceeding swift of foot, had got to the edge of the morass, where was a wide slough of mire and marsh-water, bridged with two pine-trunks laid side by side. Over this bridge flew the Wend, and I leaped from my horse (which was of no avail in such ground), meaning to follow the chase on foot. But as I did so, the heathen flung the pine-logs over into the slough, which swallowed them forthwith; and thus was all passage cut off. Then I, seeing no other way to reach him, drew my dagger, and hurled it across the slough at him with all my might; and by good hap it smote him full on the breast, so that he reeled back some three or four paces, and then fell down dead.'

An approving murmur, almost swelling into a shout, ran through the listening throng, who knew what a blow the fall of this great chief would be to the stubborn foes with whom they were contending.

Just then Geierfels happened to turn slightly; and the king and those about him saw for the first time that the baron's dagger-sheath actually *was* empty, the weapon having really fallen out into the slough as he stooped to tear up the log-bridge that was Conrad's only way of escape. This certainly bore out the story he had told; for, in the midst of that perilous region and that merciless war, no man would be likely to part with a trusty weapon without good cause.

In fact, this crafty villain, during the night, had thought well over the tale he meant to tell next day; he had devised the master-stroke of claiming as his own the exploit of the man whom he had betrayed to death, thus attaining the three-fold advantage of sweeping his hated foe from his path, usurping the credit of the latter's greatest feat, and branding the lost man's memory with undying shame.

For the time, at least, this masterpiece of baseness gained its end; for no one doubted that the baron had really slain Patkul, and the conqueror of that terrible champion was sure of a favourable hearing from all present.

'I' faith, we owe thee no small thanks, Sir Baron,' cried the king, in a much more friendly tone than before, 'for yon Patkul hath ever been a sore stumbling-block in our path. Be assured thy good deed shall not be forgotten; but now go on with thy tale, I pray, and let us hear what more befell.'

'Since thou bidd'st, lord king, I must needs speak, though I have no great mind

to it,' said the baron, with affected reluct-
ance; 'but, since the truth must be told,
I saw, as I gat me to horse again, a score
or so of the Wends coming through the
skirt of the morass, glancing backward as
men who flee from pursuit; and in their
midst was one in armour!'

The listeners all looked at Rudolf. Rudolf
looked at the speaker as if he could have
torn him limb from limb.

'At that I marvelled much,' pursued
Geierfels, 'for he bore him not like a
captive, but went among them as one that
is free, no man laying hand on him. But
his face I could not see, by reason of them
that were about him.'

The king gave a slight start, and bent
forward as if to speak, a sure sign how
utterly his wonted composure had been
overborne by the excitement of this strange
tale. But he checked himself, and settled
back into his place.

'When they espied Patkul's body,' went
on the baron, 'they set up a great cry, and
gathered round the corpse, shrieking and
making moan after their heathenish fashion;
and then, as I turned me to ride away (for
the sun was nigh unto its setting), it chanced
that he in the armour turned his face toward

me; and, as I am a living man, it was the
face of Sir Conrad of Hohenzollern!'

A sombre pause followed the utterance
of this horrible falsehood, broken at last by
the deep voice of the king himself. 'Sir
Rudolf of Hapsburg, thou hast heard the
testimony; it is for thee to reply to it on
thy kinsman's part.'

The fiery young Swiss would probably
have replied to it by knocking the slanderer's
teeth down his throat, had he obeyed his
first impulse; but happily he had the sense
to see that any violence would only harm
his cousin's cause instead of helping it.
With a mighty effort of that marvellous
self-control for which he was so famous in
after years, he choked down his righteous
wrath, and replied in the cold, measured
tones of perfect composure. 'I would fain
know what thing could have power to make
my kinsman stain his name and peril his
soul. What had he to gain—he who had
already made him a name in war, and had
been honoured with the king's favour—what,
I say, had he to gain by casting away all
this to herd with heathen savages?'

The argument was a shrewd one, and
had a visible effect on many of his hearers.
Even the baron looked nonplussed for a

moment; but he had gone too far to draw back, and replied doggedly, 'How if they were minded to make him king?'

There was a general start of amazement; but our hero said as calmly as ever, 'I' faith, a strange time for any man to wish to be king of the Wends, when their realm is overrun and laid waste, and their people trampled down by an invading host! Methinks, too, the Wends' own king, Mistevoi, and his nephew and heir, Prince Radomir, might have a word to say to that bargain.'

'Methinks thou art strangely learned in the matters of these heathen dogs, Sir Rudolf of Hapsburg,' broke in Count Valens, in a low, sneering tone, as venomous as the hiss of a snake. 'Might one make bold to ask how and whence such knowledge was gotten?'

Such insolence, from such a man, was quite too much for Rudolf's patience. But, like another famous leader of after-times, the great Hapsburg 'always kept his temper when he was *really* angry'; and the quiet, overwhelming scorn of his tone, as he replied, made every word cut like a whip: 'Deem'st thou, Sir Count, that I am in league with the heathen against mine own people? Say it plainly, and let yon worthy

baron support thy falsehood as he is wont
to do; what is one more lie to such as ye?
Thou wert not so bold of speech yester-
eve, when nought but this hand of mine
kept Radomir's steel from thy helpless
carcass, as it lay rolling in the dirt at his
feet!'

A half-stifled laugh billowed through the
whole assembly at this home-thrust at a
man who, however feared, was neither loved
nor respected. The count's coarse face grew
purple with fury, and he made a stride
forward, with hand on sword, as if to take
instant vengeance; but just then King
Ottocar made his commanding voice heard
once more: 'Sirs, this is but unprofitable
debate. We be here this day, not to brawl
or bandy bitter words, but to find out the
truth, and to do justice; and, with God's
help, so will we do. Let us to horse, and
go straight to the spot whereof Sir Otto
of Geierfels hath spoken; it may be we
shall there find somewhat to teach us how
stand the rights of this matter.'

He was promptly obeyed; and, guided
by the malignant baron (who would have
ridden fifty miles through a snowstorm for
a far smaller chance of revenge), they were
soon at the spot he had indicated. By

Ottocar's orders, three or four pine-trees that grew near the edge of the swamp were felled and laid athwart the encircling slough; and the first to cross this perilous bridge was the king himself.

'Press not forward too hastily, sirs,' said he to his knights as they flocked after him; 'in this soft earth there must needs be foot-marks, and it behoves us to take good heed not to efface them. Now, canst thou show me, Sir Otto, where Patkul stood when thy dagger smote him?'

'Here, by the edge of the slough, did it strike him, and he reeled back a pace or two, and fell as it might be here; and lo! here be the marks of his fall, even as thou seest.'

In fact, the dark, ominous stains that flecked the trampled earth at that spot told their own story; and thus, by a terrible irony of fortune, the very traces of Conrad's exploit served to transfer the credit of it to his bitterest foe.

'And the Wends bore away his body, saidst thou not?' went on the king, still looking keenly at the ground; 'and here, in truth, are their footprints——' Here he stopped short, with a sudden horror in his eyes that struck every one dumb.

Hapsburg, with a chill fear tightening round his gallant heart, such as he had never felt till then, pressed to the front, and saw the king gazing fixedly at the stained earth before him. The bare feet of the savages had dinted the soft clay deeply on every side; but in the midst of them (far too plain to leave any room for doubt) was the print of a foot cased in steel!

All looked at each other in silence, the well-wishers of Conrad in blank amazement and horror, the baron's partisans in base and cruel exultation. Ottocar, still without a word, went slowly forward, with his eyes fixed on the ground, steadily following the tracks. For ten yards or so the foot-marks of the Wends, and the print of the armed foot among them, were plainly seen; and then all the traces alike were suddenly lost amid rank weeds and long grass.

But all could see clearly, and Rudolf himself could not deny (though inwardly frantic at being forced to admit it), that there was no sign of this man in armour having been dragged along by force. Whoever he was, he had evidently walked upright, and to all appearance uncontrolled; and, as if to leave not a shred of doubt for hope to cling to, in the grass lay, just where the tracks ended, a stray helmet-plume, in which all knew the Hohenzollern colours!

'I have seen enough,' said the king gloomily; 'let us be gone!'

Back he went over the log-bridge, followed by his knights, among whom came Rudolf, in an agony of grief, rage, and rending consciousness of impotence, to which the worst tortures that his savage foes could have inflicted would have been nothing.

CHAPTER XIV.

ENSNARED.

AND where was Sir Conrad of Hohenzollern all this while?

The sullen plunge of the pine-logs into the fathomless abyss of mire below, mingling with his enemy's fiendish laugh, sounded in Conrad's ear like a death-knell. An impassable gulf on this side, a swarm of bloodthirsty savages on that; nothing was left for him but to die like a man.

The brave young Swabian commended his soul to God, and, drawing himself up defiantly, sword in hand, awaited the coming of his murderers; but instead of rushing upon him at once, the Wends, as they neared him, began visibly to hesitate.

Superstitious like all savages, these wild men saw in the fall of their redoubtable Patkul before this mere lad (coupled with the youth's firm bearing, his bright, fearless face, and look of calm defiance as he stood facing them, one against twenty) a clear proof that he must be more than mortal, and to be feared accordingly. They all knew the legend of how the martyr-bishop, St Adalbert of Prag (whom their forefathers had slain in the sacred grove) had warned his murderers that his blood would one day be avenged upon them; and what if this seeming youth were the saint himself, arisen from the grave for vengeance?

In fact, ever since this final struggle began, a mysterious and ever-deepening terror had weighed down the fierce Wendish tribesmen, chiefs and people alike. These Christians, whom they had expected to defy securely amid their swamps and forests, had marvellously overcome all resistance. The swamps had been bridged and causewayed, the forests burned to ashes, the best native warriors trampled down like grass; and, worst of all, the altar and image of their sun-god Radegast, had been overthrown and destroyed, and their formidable 'One-eyed Priest' himself all but done to death by an evil spirit— for such they fully believed Mad Matthew to be. Surely, then, the God of the Christians, in whose name such wonders had been wrought, must be stronger by far than any native god; and if this bright, saint-like youth had really been raised by Him from the dead to overthrow them, who could stand against him?

To any Wend of that age, such a marvel was not only possible, but quite natural; and before this one young lad the twenty strong, savage men paused in silent awe. Then suddenly a harsh voice was heard from the midst of the band, as a tall warrior stooped to tug from the earth a huge stone, 'If he be mortal, this will beat him down. Let us try!'

The terrible missile hurled through the air and came full on Conrad's helmet with a stunning shock; and down went the gallant boy beneath the stroke like a slender pine before the woodman's axe.

It was at that moment that the retreating Geierfels turned in his saddle to look back, just in time to see his hated foe fall, and the savages rush yelling upon him.

But, just as all seemed over, the fierce warrior who had flung the fatal stone, as he bent over the helpless knight to deal him a death-blow, was seen to start back, and to point excitedly at the fallen man's helmet, gasping in amazement, 'The necklace! the necklace!'

In fact, Conrad had fixed on his helmet, in obedience to the king's order, the bear-claw chain given him by Prince Radomir when he saved the latter from the quagmire. So long as he stood upright, the chain had been half-hidden by his helmet-plumes; but his fall left it fully visible to the fierce eyes around him, and instantly began a hubbub of startled comments.

'It is in truth Prince Radomir's chain, brothers; I know it well. And mind ye not how he told us he had given it to a smooth-faced lad, young and fair to see, even as this youth?'

'Aye, truly, comrade; and he bade us have a care of such a one if we should meet him in fight, and deal with him as a friend, and not as a foe.'

'And even so will we do,' cried the giant that had hurled the stone, who seemed to be the leader of the party. 'Forasmuch as he had our prince at his mercy, and slew him not, but saved his life and aided him to escape, may my hand wither ere it harm a hair of his head! Raise him up, lads, for he liveth yet; he is but stunned by my blow.'

One of the other Wends unclasped Conrad's helmet, and a second ran to fill it with water from a pool hard by, and began to wash away the blood that trickled from the young knight's forehead, which was fearfully bruised by the blow. Ere long the youth opened his heavy eyes, and looked round with a vacant stare.

'Fear us not, Christian; we are thy friends,' said in broken and barbarous German the tall leader, Burislav, resting on his brawny knee the young Swabian's powerless head. 'Against him who saved our great prince, Radomir, and who weareth his necklace, no man in Wend-land will lift a finger.'

While the Wend spoke, Conrad had so far come to himself as to realise what had happened, and understand what was being said. With a great effort he raised himself into a sitting posture; and as he did so, the savages around drew hastily back, as if afraid that he might spring up and bite them; for, though their terror of him as a supernatural being was somewhat quieted by his fall beneath their leader's blow, it awoke again when they saw that he was not killed after all.

'Stranger,' said Burislav, with a perceptible tremor in his strong, harsh voice, 'tell me, I pray thee, art thou indeed a mortal man, or some mighty one come down from heaven?'

Conrad could have had no doubt that if he had answered in the affirmative, his cap-

tors would have let him go at once. But,
apart from the natural repugnance of his
manly and noble spirit to deceit of any
kind, he held firmly the belief of his age,
that such a sacrilege as the assumption of
the character of a saint or angel would draw
down the instant vengeance of Heaven on
the impious deceiver.

'No heavenly one am I,' said he simply,
in tolerably fluent Wendish, 'but a mortal
man like yourselves.'

The big savage looked visibly relieved, as
did all his comrades, though they were
plainly startled at this stranger's knowledge
of their tongue.

'Glad am I,' went on Conrad, 'to have
saved your prince; for he was a brave man,
and I would fain have such men for my
friends, not for my foes. Nor think I am
come hither for mere love of blood and
rapine. I came to aid in giving peace to
this distracted land, and persuading ye all to
forsake your heathen idolatries, and to join
us, like brothers, in serving the one true God
who hath made and loved all men alike, be
they Wend or German!'

The savages looked blankly at him, and
then at each other. Here was something
new, indeed ; here was a man whose courage

they had proved—one of the hated Christians whom they regarded as their deadliest foes and destroyers—speaking of them as his fellow-men, offering to be their friend, and owning that he had risked his life to save his most formidable enemy among them.

The clear, musical voice, the fresh, boyish face, the kindly look, the frank, simple speech, went straight to the heart of these forlorn and desperate men, made doubly ferocious by defeat, ruin, and despair; and Burislav replied in a friendly and almost respectful tone, contrasting strangely with his harsh voice and grim visage, ' Were all the followers of the White Christ like thee, young chief, methinks it were no hard matter for us all to be friends and brothers as thou sayest; but though your priests have told us that He bade all men love one another, I trow the deeds of His worshippers agree but ill thereto. Howbeit, this is no time to debate such matters; for thy comrades will be upon us if we tarry longer, and we must away. Come thou with us; and though we may not let thee go free, thou shalt be as safe among us as with thine own people. Art thou yet able to stand?'

Conrad (the first stun of the blow having passed off) stoutly declared that he was, and

made good his words by rising to his feet,
and even taking a step forward.

'Well and manfully done!' cried Burislav,
touched in spite of himself by the brave
lad's resolute defiance of pain and weakness;
'thou art indeed worthy to be the friend
of Prince Radomir.'

Little dreaming of the fatal error which
those footprints of his were to cause, not
many hours later, among his own brothers-in-
arms, Conrad, with some slight aid from the
sinewy arm of his former assailant, succeeded
in walking as far as the next water-course.
Here lay, hidden in the tall reeds, two of
those rude boats in which the natives of
this amphibious region were wont to thread
its watery mazes. Conrad was hastily put
aboard one of them, and then both barks
glided away into the depths of the dismal
swamp.

CHAPTER XV.

THE LAST STRUGGLE OF HEATHENISM.

'SAY they not, my lord Sir Rudolf, that the good Bishop of Riga himself cometh hither to meet us?'

'It is so rumoured, good Andrer-Knecht; and men say the bishop hath taken ship from Riga with his train, and is faring along the coast by sea, purposing to land hard by where we are now.'

'Marry, then must we all play the man this day, for I trow this is the last stand of the heathen; and if we win the fight, it will be golden news for the good bishop, when he cometh, that there is an end of idolatry in these parts once and for ever.'

It was even as he said; that day was to decide whether heathenism or Christianity should have the mastery of East Prussia.

King Ottocar was not one to do his work by halves; and his invasion was no flying raid like those of the Poles and Brandenburgers, passing and leaving no trace behind.

It was a steady and systematic conquest, advancing step by step, and slowly but surely carrying out its purpose to the end.

In the track of the conquering host, as it rolled on, heathen and barbarous Wend-land was being shaped, little by little, into what was one day to be Christian and civilised Prussia. Sturdy Dutch spade-men were draining and planting the swampy wastes; stout Flemish and German labourers were making firm the spongy soil with cart-loads of sand and gravel; and skilled Danish carpenters were piecing together log-forts, block-houses, and even entire villages, one of which latter (named by its builders 'Wehrlin' or 'Little Rampart') is now Berlin, the capital of Germany.

Against the great king's iron tenacity, all the frantic valour of the Wends broke itself in vain. Back, back, back they were driven, foot by foot, fighting savagely for every mile of ground—back even to the very shore of the Baltic, where at length, behind the defences of their last fortress (a low sandy ridge, fortified with a triple line of palisades) the desperate men turned grimly to bay.

Ottocar's whole army had been brought up for the final struggle; for, where so much

was at stake, the king knew better than to
leave a single chance unused. He himself
commanded the centre, and Count Valens
of Thuringia the left (for, ruffian and bully
as he was, the fierce count was none the
less an approved warrior), and the right was
led by brave old Grand Master Hermann von
der Salza, with whom rode the best of his
knights.

And all this while, around these armed
thousands who were thirsting for each other's
blood, the morning sun shone in cloudless
glory, and the ripples of the blue sea danced
and sparkled in its light, and the birds
carolled blithely on the green boughs, and
the breeze murmured pleasantly through the
leaves, and all was bright and peaceful and
beautiful. But, amid all this brightness and
peace and beauty, the carnival of death was
about to begin.

Then suddenly, in that dead hush of expectation, staunch old Von der Salza, far
to the right, was seen to advance a spear-
length before the glittering line of helmets
and lances, and to bare his noble grey
head reverently, as he uttered in his deep,
sonorous voice (heard far and wide amid
that tomb-like silence) the brief, simple,
homely supplication that he was wont to

call his 'saddle-prayer,' as being always used
just before he went into battle:

> 'Christ Jesus guide us all this day,
>   And our father, above us aye;
>   Let him who stronger is than He
>   Come and try to do harm to me.'

As he ended, the air rang with the blast
of the signal-trumpets, shrilly answered by
the vulture-like scream of the Wend war-
cry; and the last battle began.

Plainly the first thing to do was to break
through or cut down the Wendish palisades;
but this was easier said than done. Burn
they would not, after the heavy rain of
the last few days; and Ottocar, who knew
better than to waste his men in a reckless
assault ere the ground was thoroughly cleared
for it, sent forward a body of sappers (as we
should call them now) to cut the piles of
the stockade at the foot, protected by his
archers and crossbowmen, who kept pouring on the defences such a hail of missiles
that not a single Wend could show his
head above the palisade without being
hit.

But the ever-watchful Radomir (who,
savage as he was, was none the less a born
general) had foreseen and provided against

this mode of attack likewise. Just within the stockade were piled large heaps of heavy stones, which the defenders, without exposing themselves to the archery, hurled with deadly force at every spot where they could hear the sappers at work.

In this way not a few of the latter were severely hurt, and several slain outright. The rest hung back, daunted; and, for the time, the central attack was completely paralysed, while on the left things were going even worse.

Count Valens, full of the rash and arrogant daring which lost so many battles in that age, boastfully declared that 'no rabble of bare-limbed savages' should ever stay *him*, and, scorning the aid of either sapper or archer, dashed at the stockade with his mounted knights and men-at-arms, hoping to break it down with the sheer weight of the charge.

But the braggart count fared no better than other leaders who despise their enemy. So much did the loose sand and uphill slope weaken the force of his rush, that it only shook the palisade without overthrowing it; and just then a large body of Wends, bursting forth from a sally-port, fell like tigers on the assailants while spent and breathless with their charge, and cut them down without mercy.

Even under this fearful disadvantage, however, the gallant Germans stood to it with all the courage of their race, and strove manfully to hold their ground. But, taken thus by surprise, and attacked in flank by thrice their number while disordered by that headlong rush over difficult ground, they had not a chance; and of the few who escaped with life, there was not one who had not his wound to show.

Count Valens and the Baron of Geierfels, cut off from the rest, hewed and slashed like furies at the ever-shifting whirl of savage faces that hemmed them in, while hurling at friend and foe alike ceaseless volleys of the curses and foul language which every gentleman of that chivalrous age had at his tongue's end. But when, by sheer dint of hacking and hammering, they at last succeeded in cutting their way through, both leaders left their gallant steeds dead behind them, and brought back hardly one in ten of their ill-fated followers. Shrill and high rose the Wends' wolfish yell of triumph, and the baffled assailants gnashed their teeth as they heard it.

A grim smile flickered over the weather-beaten faces of two stalwart men who, with the Hapsburg colours in their steel caps, were silently watching the repulse of the count's assault; and the shorter of the two said with a hoarse chuckle, 'See now, comrade Bendix, how goodly a thing it is to be a knight and a noble! Then may'st thou run thy head against a solid wall, and cast away thy men's lives, and founder thy good steed with charging uphill, and it shall be all to thy credit! Had thou or I, lad, done as yon gay count, they would have called us fools, and belike hanged us as such, if by chance we 'scaped the foeman's steel; whereas all men will cry to *him*, "Well struck! well dared! this is indeed as befits the laws of chivalry!"'

'Marry, the laws of chivalry may go hang for me, friend Andrer - Knecht,' said the shepherd-soldier with a broad grin. 'Rather would I fight, if fight I must, by the laws of common sense; and here, I trow, is a goodly chance to do it. Seest thou aught, brother, at the foot of yon palisade, in a line with that white stone?'

'That do I, in very deed,' cried the ex-robber, with sparkling eyes, 'and I wot I have oft crept through as small a gap, whether to win booty or to save my neck.'

In fact, that part of the slope which they were facing was furrowed by the channel of a dry watercourse, now all but choked with the loose, shifting sand. The palisade crossed this trench at right angles; and, just where it did so, the crumbling soil had fallen away from the piles, leaving below them a gap just wide enough to let one man pass at a time.

'These worshipful knights, I trow,' chuckled Hans, 'would deem it foul shame to lower their crests thus, and had rather die than stoop to crawl through such a hole! Well is it for thee and me, lad, that we are but poor churls, whose dignity standeth not so stiff, and who may do what "their honours" may not.'

'Not like them thinketh our master Sir Rudolf, I wot,' said Andrer-Knecht. 'Call me Saracen an' he leap not at the adventure as soon as he hears of it.'

Sure enough, Hapsburg (who had been chafing fiercely at the failure of the first assault) snatched at this chance of retrieving the day, and at once led eleven of his best men to make the attempt.

Swiftly, but cautiously, the daring men stole up the hillside toward the opening, stooping as much as they could, and even creeping at times on their hands and knees to avoid detection. More than once they actually halted and lay down among the dead that strewed the slope, fearing to be discovered ere their work was done.

But the risk of detection was really small, not only because they were quite hidden by the dust-clouds which the rising wind drove full in the faces of the defenders, but also because the latter had for the moment left that part of the stockade quite unguarded, as they hurried off to repel fresh attacks on the right and left. Bendix was the first to wriggle through the gap into the enclosure; at his heels came Andrer-Knecht, and the third was Rudolf himself.

'Now,' cried Hapsburg, springing to his feet, 'down with these piles, and make a breach for our comrades to enter.'

He suited the action to the word, and, manfully seconded by his followers, brought pile after pile crashing down.

'Help, brothers, help! they break our wall!' screamed a harsh voice on the right; and instantly a wave of wild figures, and hideous faces, and brandished weapons came bursting upon the little handful of heroes.

Then, for a few fierce moments, all was one mad whirl of stabbing, and cleaving, and slashing, and pounding. Rudolf's battered helmet clanged like a bell, his dinted shield was struck from his powerless arm, while Andrer-Knecht and Bendix, attacked by a dozen savages at once, could give him no help.

A moment more, and one of those merciless strokes might have cut short the young leader's career, and changed the whole history of Europe; but his men were as prompt to aid him as the Wends to assail. Swarming with shouts of triumph through the breach (wide enough by this time to admit three men abreast) they burst on the Wends in turn, and bore down all before them.

While this was going on, Count Valens of Thuringia, taking advantage of the enemy's confusion, renewed his attack with more judgment, and succeeded in breaking through the barrier on the left, while Salza and his knights did the same on the right. So suddenly were these three successes achieved that the defenders of the first stockade had barely time to retire into the second, while their comrades covered the retreat with a storm of arrows and stones.

But though successful thus far, the assailants had still much to do ere the day was won. It was already noon, and as yet only

one of the enemy's lines had been carried.
Two more were still to be stormed, seemingly even stronger than that which had
cost so much toil and blood. King Ottocar
himself began to look grave; and, in truth,
he well might.

Count Valens (who, to give him his due,
had risked his life as boldly as the roughest
soldier in his train) had been sorely wounded,
and carried off the field. Several of the
grand-master's knights were slain, and many
more disabled. The loss of the men-at-arms
had been immense; and the knights and
nobles, unused to fight on foot, were all but
worn-out with the weight of their armour
and the burning heat of the day.

Well might the great king be so anxious;
for the decisive success by which he had
hoped to end the war that very day seemed
as far off as ever.

The day was already far advanced, and if
the Wends could hold their ground till
night (as seemed not unlikely) they would
slip away from him in the dark as they had
done before, establish themselves in some
new fastness of that wild region, and perhaps spin out this harassing war till the
coming of the terrible northern winter drove
him home again, with his work still undone.

Come what might, that must not be; and
he gave orders for an instant assault on the
second stockade.

Just then he found himself close to a
group of men wearing the Hapsburg colours,
and said to them pleasantly, 'Ye have done
me good service this day, ye Hapsburg men;
and I——' Here he suddenly recognised
Bendix, and called out, 'Ha! thou here?
Once did thy wit outrun mine; can it now
give me any counsel whereby I may end
this battle?'

'Marry, that can it, lord king,' chuckled
the ex-shepherd. 'Seest thou not that these
archers of thine do but spend their shafts
on the palisade, and hit no man? I trow
yon Wends will all die of old age ere such
archery harm them. Bid thy men shoot
upward, that the shafts may fall on the foe
from above. Even so did I once see a
skilled hunter slay a bear that deemed itself
safe behind a rock.'

The king eagerly adopted this device (the
same by which William the Conqueror, two
centuries before, had won the battle of
Hastings), and its effect was quickly seen
in the confusion and dismay of the enemy,
of which Andrer-Knecht (who had not
been a robber for nothing, and had some

experience in breaking down barriers) was prompt to take advantage. 'Here is your key, lads,' cried he to his comrades, as he pointed to a thick pine-trunk that had been used to strengthen the captured stockade. 'Bring it forward quickly, and then

'We'll open the gates without more ado,
And let the king and his men pass through.'

With a loud laugh, the soldiers raised the pine-stem from the earth, and, forming a line, ran the tree like a battering-ram against the palisade before them. Down came half-a-dozen piles at once, with a deafening crash; and in burst Ottocar's men through the breach, himself at their head.

'Belike these be no chivalrous devices,' said Andrer-Knecht to Hans with a grim smile, as they broke into the enclosure side by side; 'but they do the work, none the less.'

As he spoke, a sudden rush of men flung him sprawling on his back, while Hans was thrown right into the arms of the king himself, with such force that king and peasant went rolling in the dirt together.

Prince Radomir, having hastily drawn together a number of his best men, had made a furious charge on the assailants while still disordered with their own success, and had borne them back to the breach, and all but forced them through it. But just as the fate of the battle wavered in the balance a second time, the grand-master's knights and men-at-arms, from the far right, came charging to the rescue.

Finding a part of the palisade before them left bare of defenders, they had clambered over it on each other's shoulders, and falling on Radomir's victorious men in flank, broke and overthrew them in turn. The Wends gave way on every side, and the second stockade was won.

But the third still remained to be surmounted, and it was the worst of all, for along its whole front bristled a tangled mass of briars, tough and pliant, too damp to be burned, giving no support to foot or hand, yet entangling any one who thrust himself into them, with meshes as strong as iron wire.

As Ottocar looked blankly at these formidable obstacles (while relieving his feelings, in the kingly fashion of the time,

with a string of curses of which a modern
house - breaker might well be ashamed)
Rudolf of Hapsburg stepped up to him,
and said a few words in an undertone.
The king started, eyed him with a look
of mingled surprise and pleasure, and then
gave an order to the nearest soldiers, which
flew from mouth to mouth along the whole
line.

Instantly hundreds of men were at work,
breaking down or tearing up the piles of
the stockade that they had just won, flinging
these up-torn logs against the still uncon-
quered palisade in front, and then coming
back for more, till the obstructing briars
were crushed flat beneath the weight, and
the piled-up logs formed a sloping ascent up
which the assailants could charge at a run.

'God is with us, comrades!' shouted Hapsburg, waving his men on. 'Forward! we
fight for the cause of Heaven!'

The words thrilled through every man
who heard them, and the rudest soldier in
the ranks felt his heart bound at the
thought that he was indeed Heaven's champion against the powers of darkness and
evil, and could do something, however little,
for the good cause.

But the assault was met as bravely as

it was made. The stubborn valour of the
modern Russian was strong in his fierce
kinsmen, who were fighting not only for
their lives, but for what they held dearer
still, the old faith of their fathers; and for
it they battled and died as bravely as the
best knight in the Christian host.

The fight was still at the hottest when
a trumpet-blast from the *sea* made both
hosts look round in amazement, just in time
to behold three small vessels gliding out
from behind one of the low sand-ridges
of the coast.

As they neared the beach, came floating
on the wind the measured chant of the
noble psalm, 'Why do the heathen so furi-
ously rage?' which had long been the battle-
hymn of the Templars in Palestine; and
then the foremost vessel was seen to heave-
to and lower a couple of boats, which, to
the dismay of the gazing Wends, were
instantly filled with shining helmets and
glittering weapons!

In reality, this was nothing more than
the good Bishop of Riga coming to join
the king according to promise; and these
armed men were only the escort without
which, in that iron age, the most peaceful
traveller never stirred abroad, however short

his journey. But so strangely do things happen sometimes, that the coming of this quiet old churchman, who had never struck a blow in his life, decided the fate of the battle. The Wends, naturally supposing that a fresh force had come up to cut off their retreat, were seized with a sudden panic, and began to give way, while Ottocar's men, with a mighty shout, swept down upon them like a wave.

Two men on the heathen side strove valiantly to stem this tide of ruin—an old man and a young one; and in the elder of the two Ottocar recognised the Wendish king, Mistevoi.

'King against king!' shouted Ottocar, rushing at him; 'let us see which is the stronger!'

His mighty sword flashed and fell, and Mistevoi fell senseless; but between the victor and his prey started up the strong arm and fierce eye of Radomir.

One smashing blow cracked the king's helmet like a hazel-nut, and beat him down to the earth as if a rock had fallen on him; but just as all seemed over, Hapsburg rushed in beneath the brandished weapon, and grappled with the Wendish champion, man to man.

They rolled on the ground together, and Rudolf felt himself crushed to the earth as if by the weight of a mountain, with a strangling clutch at his throat. Then came a dull thud close to his ear—the choking grasp relaxed — and his trusty follower, Andrer-Knecht, was bending over him, and the terrible Radomir lay motionless at his side.

'Just in time, God be praised!' said the ex-bandit, drawing a deep breath of relief as he aided his master to rise.

With that one blow Andrer-Knecht ended the battle. Even those of the Wends who had not seen Radomir fall seemed to feel instinctively the loss of their guiding spirit, and gave way on every side. Brave Burislav, disdaining to save himself by flight, fell by an unknown hand, fighting to the last; and when the good old Bishop of Riga and his train at length came ashore, they found the Christian banners already waving in triumph over the last battlefield of heathen Wendland.

CHAPTER XVI.

THE THREE-HEADED IDOL.

WHEN Conrad of Hohenzollern was borne off by the savages, he was at first too much stunned by what had befallen to make any attempt to consider his position; and, in truth, so sudden and terrific a disaster might well make the stoutest heart fail. At one moment free, happy, victorious; in the next, betrayed, wounded, captive among pitiless savages.

Nor had he, to all appearance, anything better to expect than a violent and hideous death; for he had small faith in the assurances of his captors that his life was safe, especially when he recalled their custom of slaughtering all prisoners as a sacrifice to their idols.

But he soon became incapable of connected thought of any kind; for, now that the first numbness of the blow that had felled him was beginning to pass off, it was followed by a rending pain, which disabled him from thinking at all, or even taking any notice of his surroundings.

Meanwhile the Wendish canoes, skilfully paddled, glided on through the dreary waste, now brushing an overhanging curtain of wild grass, now crunching through a forest of huge reeds, now skimming over a dark, still, slimy pool (from which a cloud of insects rose as they passed) and anon threading a maze of shallow, muddy, unending lagoons, where no other boat could have passed, and no other boatman found his way.

As the red sunset faded over the weird desolation of the boundless fen, and the reedy banks and bush-clad islets melted into the ghostly dimness of night—amid a tomb-like silence broken only by the faint plash of the paddles or the shriek of some passing night-bird—the wounded knight's fevered fancy recalled the 'death-boat' gravely declared by Byzantine historians to ferry nightly across the Strait of Dover, to a world of shadows beyond, the souls of all who had died that day; and he could even call to mind the very words in which a passing student had once told him the wild legend:

'Opposite the shore of Gaul, but separated by an arm of the sea, lies a ghastly region, on which clouds and tempests brood for ever, and where the ground is covered with snakes; and thither the spirits of the departed are sent after death. On the Gaulish shore of the strait dwell a few fishermen, who, performing the office of the heathenish Charon, ferry over nightly to this isle of eternal darkness the spirits of all who have died that day. In the dead of night a knock, given by no mortal hand, is heard at the door of the ferryman's hut, and a whisper as of a dying breeze summons him to his duty. No sooner has he launched his bark than he sees it sink sensibly in the water with the weight of the dead; but no form is seen, and, though voices are heard, the accents are as of one who speaks in his sleep.'

At last both boats came to a sudden halt; and the exhausted captive was lifted out on the bank in a kind of stupor, half sleep and half swoon.

When he came to himself again, it was broad daylight; and he found that he had been relieved of his armour, and was lying on a heap of dried grass in the corner of a reed hut, while over him bent a wrinkled, gap-toothed old woman, ugly enough for

any witch of German legend, who offered
him a horn filled with some dark liquid.

Parched with thirst, the young man drank
eagerly. Whether from the effect of the
potion or from sheer weakness, he almost
instantly became unconscious once more;
and at his next awakening he found himself alone in the hut, through the half-open
door of which streamed the red glow of
sunset.

Walking to the door, he saw that he was
on an islet of some size in the midst of the
morass, dotted with similar huts, before
which sat groups of women and children,
mingled with a few old men; and he rightly
guessed this to be one of the camps of
refuge where the Wends left their non-
combatants, while the fighting-men were in
the field against the invader.

All at once a child from the nearest
group, espying the stranger in the doorway,
ran forward, with the fearless curiosity of
childhood, to have a closer view of him.
Conrad, naturally fond of children, soon
made friends with the tiny Slavonian, whose
grandfather, after eyeing him doubtfully
from a distance for a moment or two, came
up and greeted him in turn; and then all
three (Conrad leading the child by the

hand) went to join the group whence it had strayed.

The Wends (who evidently knew all about his rescue of their great prince, and the token of friendship given him by the latter) received him very kindly; and in a trice he was seated among them with little Radegonda in his lap, partaking of the food that his new friends hastened to set before him, and telling them, in the intervals of his meal, the tale of his romantic meeting with Prince Radomir.

So well, in fact, did the brave lad adapt himself to this new and strange turn of fortune, that, by the evening of the next day, he had already (aided by his knowledge of the language) made friends with every one in the islet. But whatever pleasure he might have felt at this unlooked-for change of his worst foes into friends, and of his captivity into hospitable entertainment, was blotted out by the harrowing thought that, while he sat idle there, his brother-soldiers were fighting for their lives against the heathen.

Fain would he have made his escape; but how was he to do it? Boat he had none, and the sloughs of half-liquid mire that shut him in on every side were not

to be crossed either by leaping or swimming;
and even could he get clear of the islet,
how was he to find his way out of that
pathless swamp, and what chance would
he have in such a place without weapons
or armour?

But a change was in store for him, such
as he little expected.

It was the evening of his sixth day on
the islet, and he was seated in front of his
hut, which he had all to himself, his food
being brought by the same old woman who
had tended him at first. His little pet,
Radegonda, perched on his knee as usual,
was playing with the famous bear-claw
chain, which had been shifted from Conrad's
helmet to his neck; and her grandfather,
seated by the young Swabian's side, was
relating a wild tale of how the king of the
earth-dwarfs appeared to St Knud of Den-
mark, and gave him an enchanted cup of
fairy gold.

The young knight was listening with
much interest to the strange tale (every
word of which he firmly believed) when,
all at once, he saw a *face* rise slowly
above the edge of the bank in front of him,
hideous enough to have passed for that of
the dwarf-king in the old man's weird

legend—a lean, dark, wolfish face, lighted by the gleam of a single eye, in which shone a glare of infernal malice worthy of the demon whom the startled Conrad for a moment took this horrible apparition to be.

In truth, it *was* a demon, as cruel, and treacherous, and malignant as any goblin of Wendish legend; for the face was that of the One-eyed Priest!

Slowly the terrible man advanced toward the doomed captive, followed by four other figures as wild and sinister as his own, whom the ghastly badges that they bore showed to be members of the same grim priesthood as himself. He waved his lean brown hand, and instantly his attendants sprang upon Conrad, bound him hand and foot, and began to drag him toward the boat that had brought them thither.

A great clamour arose at once, seemingly in protest against such violence to Prince Radomir's friend and deliverer. But, as may be supposed, the high-priest's authority bore down all objection; and in a trice Hohenzollern found himself in the boat, and gliding swiftly away into the fast-falling gloom of night. The last thing he heard was poor little Radegonda crying bitterly at the loss of her new friend, and it was

characteristic of this brave lad that his
little playmate's grief moved him far more
than any anxiety as to his own case, hopeless as it seemed.

On, on, on glided the boat and her
spectral crew, turning and winding through
the lonely wilds of the great swamp, till at
last, just as utter darkness set in, they halted
on the edge of a dense pine-wood. Here
Conrad, still bound, was lifted ashore, and
laid on a kind of hurdle; this two of his
captors bore along between them at a brisk
pace, while the two others walked one on
each side, and the priest Adinglas himself
headed the party.

Even in broad day few men could have
found their way through that pathless forest.
But, dark as it was, these wild men seemed
to know the way by instinct; and in spite
of their burden, they moved onward as
swiftly and untiringly as the wolves that
they so much resembled.

At length, after a march so long that
Conrad's bearers had relieved each other
twice over, they came to a sudden halt;
he felt himself lifted from the hurdle, and
carried, as it seemed (for he could see
nothing) into a house of some kind; his
bonds were removed—a low voice said near

him, 'There is food for him here'—and then came the sound of a door being shut and barred, and he was alone.

His first idea was naturally to get some notion of his surroundings. Groping about his prison, he found it a log-hut of no great size, with a heap of dried grass and fern in one corner, and in another some dried fish and an earthen jar of water.

Satisfied that, had his gaolers meant to kill him at once, they would not have taken the trouble to feed him, the brave young Swabian made a hearty meal, and then, lying down on his rude couch, was fast asleep in a moment.

In this hut Conrad remained a close prisoner for the next two days, the walls being of stout pine-logs instead of brittle reeds, and he having no weapon with which to cut through them. Nor could it have availed him if he had, for the occasional mutterings that were heard outside told him that he was constantly watched by two guards at least, if not more.

All this time he had no communication whatever with his captors. Once in the day his door was opened slightly, and a gaunt brown hand thrust in food and water, but this was done without a word, and when he spoke he received no reply. All he could do was to keep watch through a chink between two of the logs, which he had somewhat enlarged by picking out the paste of clay and dried leaves that served as mortar. Through this peep-hole he made out that about twenty other huts stood round his, on a small clearing in the forest; and the place seemed to be a kind of colony of the heathen priests, for every one who went by wore the priestly badge.

But he saw more than this. He noticed that men were constantly passing to and fro with excited looks and gestures—that messengers were sent out ever and anon, as if to reconnoitre—and that they always came back much graver than they went.

Conrad was at no loss to interpret these signs, knowing as he did that the sweep of the king's advance was gradually penning the Wends between his army and the sea. The decisive battle must be just at hand, if not actually being fought at that moment —a galling thought to the captive knight, though he happily knew nothing of the frightful suspicion cast on him by Geierfels's infamous plot, the least hint of which would have driven him to distraction.

The red glow of sunset was fading from

tree-top after tree-top as the gathering
gloom crept on; and Conrad, with a heavy
heart, was gazing wearily through his chink
of observation, when he saw all at once
something that made even *his* bold heart
stand still. In the ghostly shadow of the
pines, just opposite to him, appeared for a
moment (vanishing instantly as if it had
never been) the tall gaunt form, spectral
visage, and restless, glittering eyes of Mad
Matthew!

Could it be really he? Conrad would
have thought himself the sport of his own
excited fancy, but for a sudden shriek of
'The demon! the demon!' from the Wends
outside, who started back and huddled
together for a moment like frightened sheep.
Then two or three of the boldest, shaking
off their panic, rushed into the thicket in
quest of the supposed phantom; but no
one was there.

There was little sleep for Hohenzollern
that night. Had Matthew really found him
out, and were King Ottocar's men at hand
to save him? At all events the behaviour
of the Wends proved that it *was* Matthew
whom he had seen; and this unhoped-for
link with the brave comrades from whom
he had been so strangely cut off did more

to raise his drooping spirits than anything else could have done.

But the first words that he heard next morning, uttered in the raven-croak of the One-eyed Priest, made his heart sink once more: 'This day will the last fight be fought. Go quickly, ye four, and see how the battle goeth, and bring me word again.'

It had come at last, then; and the final struggle was being fought out, evidently at no great distance, while he lay there, captive and helpless!

All that day the captive within and the captors without waited in feverish anxiety for the news on which hung the fate of Wend-land. Night was already falling when three of the four messengers (for of the fourth there was no sign) came tottering into the village, haggard, gasping, and smeared with dust and blood.

'All is lost!' panted the foremost, as he sank exhausted on the ground.

Then the second, taking up the fearful story, told that the hated Christians had triumphed, that the last Wendish fortress had been taken and destroyed, their best warriors killed or captured, and King Mistevoi and Radomir seriously wounded.

The savage high-priest snarled out a

curse that made even his ferocious comrades recoil, and waved his hand, with a gesture of horrible menace, towards the prisoner's hut. Instantly the door was flung open, and Conrad, seized and bound once more, was blindfolded with a skin cloak, and then lifted from the ground and borne away at a rapid pace.

All at once he felt himself set down again; the cloak that muffled his face was loosened; he heard a sound of retreating steps, and, flinging off the muffler with a violent jerk of his head, found himself alone.

At first he was at a loss to tell where he could be, for he could make out nothing but a shadowy mass of trees shutting him in on every side. But presently the first pale gleam of the rising moon showed him a huge dim form towering above him, bearing some distorted likeness to human shape, but deformed, brute-like, and hideous, beyond the power of words to convey.

Though he had never seen this hobgoblin before, Conrad had heard it described too often not to recognise it at a glance. It was the image of Triglaf, the Wends' three-headed idol!

CHAPTER XVII.

UNDER THE SACRIFICIAL KNIFE.

IN a moment the whole truth flashed upon the doomed captive. He was to be murdered as a sacrifice to the same idol before which St Adalbert had been hewn in pieces two centuries and a half before; and this gloomy wood was the 'Romova' or sacred grove that had been the scene of that famous tragedy; it was the place which he and his cousin Rudolf had vowed to penetrate, on the chaplain's assurance that he who could enter it, and overthrow the idol, should make an end of heathenism in Wend-land.

How well he remembered that vow, and the thrill of enthusiasm with which he had uttered it! and now, by a terrible irony of fortune, he *had* entered the famous grove, not to conquer, but to die!

Conrad's first thought was to free himself from his bonds; for, though he had no hope of escape, his bold spirit revolted against the idea of being butchered like a

sheep, without an attempt to resist. But
he was too securely bound, and all his
efforts were vain.

Presently back came the men who had
carried him thither, with Adinglas himself
at their head; and then followed, by twos
and threes, the whole population of the
village, till nearly a hundred people were
gathered round the idol.

Then Adinglas, as high-priest, fired a
huge pile of dry pine-wood in front of the
monstrous image; and as the fitful glare
gave a weird show of life to his three
deformed heads and staring eyes, or played
over the wild faces and tattooed or painted
bodies of his worshippers, Conrad could have
fancied himself at some midnight revel
of the wood-demons in whom he firmly
believed.

And all this while, slowly, calmly,
brightly, the glory of the full moon crept
up over the black whispering tree-tops,
gazing down on that carnival of furies with
its pure and peaceful light, before which
the lurid glare of the sacrificial fire seemed
to shrink ashamed.

'Ha! how lik'st thou the welcome we
have prepared for thee, Christian viper?'
cried one of the lesser priests, as he bent

over the helpless captive with the grin of a
hyæna. 'Thou shalt have thy fill of steel
and fire ere long, be assured of that!'

'I care not,' said the young hero firmly.
'My people have won the victory, and God
will give me strength to die!'

'Silence, dog!' roared the savage, furious
at this defiance; and he dealt the helpless
lad a cruel blow in the face. The young
knight's hot southern blood boiled at the
brutal insult; but he restrained himself with
a mighty effort, and answered never a word.

Just then, happily for him, his enemy's
attention was drawn away by the high-
priest himself, who, taking his stand before
the mound on which the idol stood, in the
full glare of the fire, uplifted his bony,
claw-like hands, and began to chant, in a
low, measured tone, a kind of invocation
that may be paraphrased as follows:

'We call on thee, Triglaf,
The master of might,
The lord of three faces,
Of terror and night.

The off'ring thou lovest
We give as thy due,
The blood of the foeman
Thy people who slew.

> The Christian invader
> Hath trampled thy sod;
> Rise, father, and save us,
> For thou art our god!'

His voice rose to a perfect shriek at this
last appeal, which all the other priests
answered with a clamour so terrific that
it went pealing far and wide through the
dim aisles of that gloomy forest, echoing
and re-echoing as if it would never end.
But as with Baal and his priests of old, so
it was now: 'there was no voice, nor any
to answer, nor any that regarded.'

Then, amid the sombre silence that followed this uproar, rang out a scornful laugh
from the doomed Swabian.

'Dost thou mock us, accursed caitiff?'
howled the One-eyed Priest, turning, knife
in hand, on the helpless prisoner, with a
scowl of infernal malice. 'Thou, at least,
art in our power, and we will show thee
no mercy. Where is thy God now, whelp
of the Christian wolves? Call on Him to
save thee if He can.'

'If He will,' replied the gallant lad, as
fearlessly as ever, 'He can save me even
now.'

The priest answered with a fiendish laugh,
and raised his knife to strike.

A twang—a whiz—a sharp cry—and the savage priest sank dead across his intended victim, while his ferocious comrades fell right and left around him. At the same moment a thundering shout of 'Hapsburg to the rescue!' made the air ring, and Rudolf himself, with a hundred stout soldiers at his back, came bursting into the fatal circle.

The savages would fain have fled; but, surprised and hemmed-in as they were, they had not a chance of escape. In a few moments all was over; and Rudolf, having dashed down the idol into the fire with one mighty stroke as he passed, was severing his cousin's bonds, and raising him to his feet again.

'I thank thee, cousin,' said the young Hohenzollern faintly.

'Thank not me, kinsman, but Matthew, whom thou shalt see presently. He it was who brought us word of thy peril, and guided us hither; and if thou standest here a living man, it is his doing, and none of mine.'

'I am much beholden to ye both,' said Conrad; 'and I give thee joy, cousin, that thou hast made good thy vow, and achieved the adventure of the idol grove. Little weened we, I trow, when thou and I took that vow upon us, in what wise it should be fulfilled.'

'To God be the glory, not to me,' said Hapsburg modestly; 'and may He grant that it be as our good chaplain hath said, and that the overthrow of the foul image that crackleth in yon flame be in very deed the end of heathendom in this land.'

The young crusador had his wish; for that night's work was the deathblow of heathenism in Wend-land. The powerlessness of the false gods to protect either their worshippers or themselves had been made fully and terribly manifest, by a proof that no one could mistake; and the spell of the old pagan belief was broken for ever.

King Mistevoi and Prince Radomir, when they recovered from the wounds received in the final battle, at once adopted the new faith. The old king even went so far as to act as interpreter to the Christian missionaries who preached to his people; and when, in the fulness of time, Radomir was left sole ruler of Wend-land by his uncle's death, he reigned as a Christian king over a Christian land.

CHAPTER XVIII.

FIRE FROM HEAVEN.

'WHERE is our trusty Matthew, Cousin Rudolf?' asked Hohenzollern, as he chafed his benumbed limbs to remove the stiffness left by his bonds. 'Fain would I thank him for the life he hath saved.'

'We will go seek him; but first put thou on thine armour, cousin, which lieth here ready to thy hand. Yon heathen rogues had hung it on these trees for a trophy to that scarecrow god of theirs; but I trow it is destined to a better end than that. So! now thou look'st like thine own self again; and now to find our good Matthew.'

But hardly had they gone a dozen paces, when Rudolf caught sight of his trusty henchman, Andrer-Knecht, kneeling by a prostrate man.

'How now, lad?' cried Rudolf; 'whom hast thou got there?'

'We have lost a trusty guide and a stout comrade, my lord,' said the ex-bandit sadly, 'for here lies Mad Matthew, slain.'

'Slain, say'st thou?' echoed Rudolf, starting as if stung; 'it cannot be.'

But his face fell as he bent over the fallen man; for, though life still lingered, his wounds were such as to leave small hope of recovery.

'Bring up the horses quickly,' said Hapsburg, in a voice that he vainly tried to steady. 'If we can but get him to the camp alive, it may be we shall save him yet, for men say yon good bishop is himself a skilled leech' (doctor).

It was well for Conrad that their ride to the camp was a short one, his strength being all but spent; but Rudolf rode beside him and held his bridle, and installed his cousin in his own tent when they reached the camp, giving strict orders to his men to say nothing of Hohenzollern's reappearance.

How well they kept the secret was shown by a striking proof on the following afternoon; for, as he was returning to his tent, the Baron of Geierfels swaggered past Rudolf with a look of insolent scorn, evidently without the least suspicion that the victim of his foul treachery still lived to denounce it, and was close to him at that very moment.

Entering the tent, Rudolf found, with

joyful surprise, his cousin so refreshed and strengthened by a quiet sleep of several hours (which was just what he needed) as to seem quite his old self once more.

But not so well did it fare with poor Matthew. The good old bishop (who, as Rudolf had said, had no mean skill in surgery) did his utmost, but all in vain; and the cousins had barely ended a long private conference, over which both looked much graver than usual, when a soldier came to tell them that Matthew was dead.

'And our lord the king hath sorrowed much for him,' added the man, 'and hath given command that the body shall be wrapped in a fair linen cloth, and laid in a tent hard by his own; and on the morrow shall it be buried with all honour.'

That night the grand-master and the Bishop of Riga supped in the king's tent, the only other persons present being Rudolf of Hapsburg, who waited on Ottocar himself, Sigismund of Altenburg, who served the grand-master, and two of the bishop's train.

'A health to our followers, high or low, who have aided in this good work!' cried the king, who seemed in high spirits. 'We have hunted down these heathen wolves at last; and in memory of it shall be built, here where we sit, a fortress that shall be named after me "Königs-Berg"' (King's Hill).

But the words died on his tongue at sight of the starting eyes and quivering lips of the grand-master, whose bold, manly face was suddenly frozen into a stare of blank and stony horror. The king turned hastily round, and beheld a sight that struck him dumb.

In the doorway of the tent stood the 'dead' Matthew, in his long white shroud; but his face, though gaunt and corpse-like as ever, had lost its crazy flightiness, and now wore a look of strange and solemn dignity, matching well with the gloomy emphasis of his tone as he said, 'Beware, O king, of pride and jealousy, and cast them speedily out of thy heart, or they will yet be thy ruin, and thou wilt lose thy life by the same hand that saved it!'

And, as the last word was uttered, the speaker, without moan or struggle, fell forward on his face, a dead man.

There was no more revelling that night. All who had witnessed the scene fully believed this last effort of expiring nature to have been an actual rising from the dead;

and the merry party broke up in confusion and terror.

When the king appeared next morning, his soldiers (who had already heard a dozen different versions of this startling event) were at no loss to account for his gloomy brow and troubled look; but they only divined half the truth. His jealous displeasure at Rudolf's brilliant exploit in the idol grove made the sinister prophecy that he should die by Hapsburg's hand fall on prepared soil; and in that hour were sown the seeds of that fatal suspicion which was one day to bear such terrible fruit.

The first duty of the day was poor Matthew's burial, the bishop himself reciting the funeral prayers; and then the king proceeded to confer honours on all who had distinguished themselves in the final conflict.

Rudolf's trusty henchman, Andrer-Knecht, donned the silver spurs of an esquire, no small promotion for a private soldier in that age. Rudolf himself, having saved the king's life, received a gold chain from Ottocar's neck, bestowed, however, with a coldness so marked as to be noticed and wondered at by all who saw it.

Hans Bendix, as the first to enter the enemy's lines, was praised and rewarded as

he deserved; and after several others had
been similarly recompensed, Ottocar called
up the Baron of Geierfels, who, brute as
he was, had, to give him his due, done
manfully in the last onset.

But ere the king could speak, he saw
the fierce baron's coarse red face suddenly
turn pale as death, and his eyes fix themselves in a stare of blank and helpless terror.
A single figure had just stepped forth from
the Hapsburg troop, and, flinging off the
long cloak that muffled it, revealed the pale
and haggard face of what the conscience-
stricken villain fully believed to be the
ghost of his victim, Conrad of Hohenzollern!

For a moment or two no one spoke or
moved; the whole multitude seemed turned
to stone. Then Conrad's voice was heard,
terribly distinct amid that dead and gloomy
silence, 'Traitor and murderer, dost thou
know me again? Well is it said that a
guilty conscience needeth no accuser.'

'What means this?' asked the king, who
began to realise that it was no ghost with
whom he had to deal, but a living man.
'Right glad am I, Sir Conrad of Hohenzollern, to find thee still alive; and if
thou hast suffered wrong, tell thy tale

boldly, and be assured that justice shall be done.'

And Conrad told, in a few simple words, his fearful story.

But Geierfels (whom this sudden and terrific disclosure had fairly paralysed for the moment) was roused by sheer desperation to all his wonted energy. He saw plainly that it was now a struggle to the death; and, rallying all his courage to face it, he flatly denied the charge, and (as usual in such cases) offered to make good his denial in single combat with his accuser.

Such combats were then held to be a direct appeal to the judgment of Heaven, and no one ever thought of doubting that whichever of the two combatants was in the right would be the one to win. The king, therefore, assented at once, and the minor details were quickly settled.

The place chosen for the fight was the spot where they stood, and the time next morning at sunrise; and as the crumbling and broken soil, honeycombed with rabbit-burrows, forbade the usual encounter on horseback, lance to lance, it was arranged that they should meet on foot, with no weapons but their swords.

Fully half an hour before the appointed

time the barrier of the lists (which had been staked-in as soon as there was light enough to do it) was lined with an unbroken hedge of jostling shoulders and eager faces. But the superstitious spectators noted with secret awe that the day was gloomy and lowering, and that the beams of the rising sun looked wan and ghastly as they struggled through the huge black cloud that was fast darkening the eastern sky.

'This bodes no good,' said one of the men-at-arms, in a hoarse whisper. 'When the sky lowers over two who meet under shield, one of those two is doomed to die!'

Hardly had he spoken when the ever-mounting blackness swallowed up the sun as if it had never been, and a pale gleam of lightning quivered for a moment along the horizon, and was gone.

Suddenly a flourish of trumpets announced the appearance of the king, who took his seat right in front of the lists. Just as he did so a fierce red glare broke through the deepening gloom overhead, and a long roll of thunder told that the coming storm was just upon them.

A moment later the two combatants entered the lists from opposite sides, attended by their 'god-fathers,' or seconds, as we should now call them—Conrad, advancing with his usual bright and fearless look, and Geierfels with the sullen ferocity of a trapped bear.

Hapsburg and the baron's second, having examined as usual the weapons and armour of the two knights, to make sure that neither had any undue advantage, drew back a pace or two, while the grand-master, as marshal of the lists, came forward in turn to administer the customary oath to the combatants.

Hohenzollern, holding up his sword-point to the sky, took the oath with his wonted cheerful confidence, though his voice was all but drowned by the uproar of the storm, which had now burst in all its fury; thunder-clap followed thunder-clap, like the cannonade of a great battle, while the lightning flamed and flared till the whole sky seemed ablaze.

But when the guilty baron (to whom this strange storm appeared sent to avenge his treachery) held up his blade in turn, the hand that grasped it trembled visibly; and it was in vain that he strove to steady the low, hoarse tone in which he uttered what was, in his case, a mere blasphemous mockery: 'I swear—so help me God and all the holy saints—that I have spoken the truth, and that the cause which I maintain is just and right; and, if it be not so, may fire from heaven——'

That impious perjury was never completed. There came a blaze of lightning that set the whole sky on fire, and a thunder-clap that seemed to shake the very earth; and when the dazzled spectators were able to look up once more they saw the baron stretched on the earth, a blackened, shrivelled corpse.

CHAPTER XIX.

THE MONK'S PROPHECY COMES TRUE.

YEARS had passed since that memorable day, and the night of the first of October 1273 was slowly darkening over the old Swiss town of Basel, and the white tents of the besieging army that compassed it about.

It was a chill, gloomy, stormy night. The rising wind moaned through the skeleton boughs of the leafless trees, the rushing Rhine glimmered faintly amid the deepening darkness, a few heavy drops of rain fell sullenly from the great black void overhead, and the sentinels of the besieging force stamped their feet for warmth as they paced to and fro and longed for their dreary watch to end.

Just as the last gleam of the red and angry sunset was fading from the slowly darkening sky, a young esquire, who had been scouting to the eastward with twenty troopers, came riding leisurely toward the beleaguering camp. He was just in sight of it when a quick tramp of approaching hoofs made him turn sharply round and couch his lance with the air of a man who meant business. 'Stand! who goes there?' he called out in a challenging tone.

'I am Friedrich of Hohenzollern, Burg-Graf of Nürnberg,' replied a deep voice out of the fast-falling darkness, 'and I have an errand to the captain of your host, Sir Rudolf of Hapsburg.'

'Well met, noble sir,' cried the young officer, in a tone of joyful surprise; 'assuredly your Excellency will be a welcome guest among us if, as men say, you come to stand umpire in my master's quarrel with this prince-bishop whom we are beleaguering here; for, in sooth, we are all well aweary of this slow siege.'

'That can I well believe,' laughed the new-comer; 'but I trust my coming may be of some avail to end the dispute.'

He spoke with the off-hand air of one dismissing a subject of no importance; and a far keener observer than this young esquire could have found nothing in the burg-graf's light tone and careless laugh to suggest that he came not merely to settle a trifling dispute between two petty local magnates, but to open a new chapter in the history of the world.

In truth, it was full time for a change
of some kind; for those were evil days for
all peoples from the Danube to the Rhine.
A violent and shameful death had cut off
in the flower of his youth the last of the
famous house of Hohenstaufen, whose great
founder had been wont to proclaim daily,
'Ho! every one that hath suffered wrong,
let him come to me, and he shall find
justice.' For years past there had been no
emperor to watch over the chaos of jarring
principalities which is now, thank God, a
united Germany at last; and in every part
of the distracted region, brutal and ignorant
barons of the Geierfels type were ruling
like petty kings, and doing that which was
right in their own eyes, and wrong in those
of everyone else.

In a word, the universal lawlessness and
misery of that iron time was not a whit
overstated by the rude rhyme which was
then in the mouth of every peasant in
Rhineland:

> To Thee, O Lord, we poor folk make moan,
> For Satan his seeds in this land has sown;
> To guard Thy children, Thou 'st set up law,
> But where is it now, these robbers to awe?

In the midst of the camp which the
burg-graf and his attendant knights were

just entering with the scouting party was
seated, before a tent as plain as the rest,
a tall man in steel-grey armour. Though
still in the prime of life, his fine face wore
the thoughtful and somewhat melancholy
gravity of one who had wrought and suffered
beyond the measure of ordinary men; and
so he had, in truth, for he was no other
than Rudolf of Hapsburg.

Around him stood several of his knights,
and in front of the group were gathered a
number of men-at-arms, two of whom held
fast between them a pale and trembling
man, so overcome by fear that, without
their support, he would at once have fallen
to the ground.

But, in fact, this poor wretch had only
too good cause for his terror. He was a
spy from the besieged town, who had just
been detected and seized by the soldiers;
and, his real character being known, he had
nothing better to expect than to be put to
a lingering and horrible death, with all the
cold-blooded and infernal cruelty for which
the 'good old times' were so justly famous.

Rudolf, with a glance of half-contemptuous
pity at the shivering coward, was just opening his lips to say what was to be done
with him, when the young esquire in com-

mand of the scouting party came hastily up, and said to him, 'My lord, your kinsman Friedrich of Hohenzollern, Burg-Graf of Nürnberg, desireth speech with you.'

'Welcome, good cousin!' cried Hapsburg, springing to his feet as the burg-graf's stately figure came forward into the circle of light cast by the camp-fire; 'in sooth it is long since we met. How fares it, I pray, with our kinsman Conrad of Hohenzollern, my brother-in-arms of old against the northern heathen?'

'He is well, and I trow thou wilt see him ere long,' said his cousin gravely; 'but ere I say more, it befits that I acquit me of a duty which I owe.'

And, suddenly kneeling on one knee before the wondering Rudolf (an example followed at once by his four knights), the burg-graf said solemnly, in a voice loud enough to be heard by all present: 'I, Friedrich von Hohenzollern, Burg-Graf of Nürnberg, and these my knights here present, do homage to thee, Rudolf, Kaiser of the Holy Roman Empire, and pledge our loyalty and knightly faith to be ever ready to do thee such service as Christian men may, God helping us. Amen.'

During this strange address Hapsburg

gazed blankly at the speaker and his kneeling knights, and said at last, in the impatient
tone of a man vexed at some ill-timed joke,
'Jest not with me, I pray thee, kinsman;
for, in truth, I have at this time neither
mind nor leisure for such May-day pranks
as these.'

'Nor have I,' said his cousin gravely;
'nor do I jest with thee, kinsman. It is
even as I have said; the estates of the
realm, deeming it full time that the griefs
of this land should be amended, have chosen
thee for their emperor, and I am the first
to do thee homage.'

The stupefied silence that followed this
astounding disclosure was suddenly broken
by a howl of terror from the captive spy,
who naturally concluded (and with but too
good reason) that whatever tortures might
have awaited him at the hands of a simple
general would certainly be tripled in honour
of the dignity of a new emperor.

Bursting from his two guards (who had
relaxed their hold of him in their first
surprise at the burg-graf's startling announce-
ment) the terrified wretch flung himself at
the new kaiser's feet, and hugged them with
the energy of desperation. 'Mercy, mercy,
mighty kaiser!' he whined; 'I but did my

master's bidding. Crush not a helpless man
—let not the first act of thy reign be a
deed of vengeance!'

The last words went straight to Rudolf's
gallant heart; and with the sudden recol-
lection of the old monk's half-forgotten
prophecy (now so strangely fulfilled) came
back to him the memory of the two deeds
of mercy with which his career had begun,
and of his unconsciously prophetic declaration
that, were he the emperor, such cruelties as
he had then witnessed should be ended once
for all.

'So be it,' he said, 'I give thee thy life;
for, as thou say'st, thou hast but done thy
master's bidding, and he, I wot well, cares
nought for other men's lives so that his own
be safe. Hearken now,' he went on with
stern impressiveness, 'go back to thy
master the prince-bishop, and tell him that
I, the Emperor of the Romans, summon
him to submit himself and his town to my
mercy, and to make amends for the wrongs
he hath done to divers of my vassals; and
tell him, farther, that if he yield not this
very night I will burn the town over his
head, and put to the sword every man of
the garrison. And now begone.'

The trembling prisoner did not need to

be told twice, and vanished as if the earth
had swallowed him.

'I' faith, fair cousin,' whispered the burg-
graf with a grim smile, 'thou tak'st as
kindly to the imperial tone as if thou had
been born a kaiser.'

No one who knows what manner of man
Hapsburg was can suppose that he really
meant to carry out these savage menaces.
But he probably calculated (and not without
reason) that the mere threat would be enough
for his blustering foe, who, like other bullies,
was wont to collapse when faced stoutly.

Without any direct reply to his cousin's
jest, Rudolf said aloud, 'Come into my
tent, Cousin Fritz, and share a soldier's
supper; and do thou, Sir Andrer-Knecht,'
he added to a stalwart man behind him,
whose red hair was thickly streaked with
grey, 'see that these four noble knights be
cared for as befits their rank and worth.'

'Andrer-Knecht?' echoed the burg-graf,
looking curiously after the red-haired man
as he led the knights away. 'Is this, then,
that famous robber of thine, to whom (as
our cousin Conrad hath told me) thou didst
once preach peace by breaking his pate?'

'He and no other,' said the new emperor,
smiling; 'and better servant no man ever

had. With mine own hand I made him a
knight, and right well did he deserve it;
and, robber though he hath been, far rather
would I trust my poor peasants in his care
than in that of yon wolf in sheep's clothing'
(and he glanced towards the town) 'who
calls himself a bishop, forsooth!'

As they sat at table there came faintly
to their ears, from time to time, the joyous
shouts with which Rudolf's soldiers (who
idolised their leader) were hailing the news
of his exaltation.

'Methinks, good cousin,' said Hapsburg,
as he listened to the far-off cheers, 'it is
to thee that my thanks are due for this
new dignity of mine, for well I wot thou
must have had no small share in bringing
it to pass.'

'I did what I could,' said the other
modestly; 'but he who did best for thy
cause was the good Archbishop of Mainz,
who hath ever had a kindness for thee since
thou didst save him from certain villains
who beset him among the hills, and then,
having sheltered him in thy castle for the
night, didst give him escort to a safe place
on the morrow.'

'Even so did it befall,' said Rudolf, after
a moment's thought, 'though in truth I

had well-nigh forgotten it. Little weened
I then that he would one day repay in
such-wise that small kindness of mine.'

'Even a small kindness is never cast
away,' cried his cousin heartily, 'though I
wot well, kinsman, thou didst it with no
thought of being repaid. But if thou wilt
walk by my counsel, be thou ware of one
who, if I err not greatly, is minded to repay
thee in far other fashion.'

'Who is he?' asked Rudolf, with a sudden
darkening of his noble face.

'Who but thine own leader in Wend-
land, King Ottocar of Bohemia! Marry, it
was as goodly a sport as any Christmas
mumming to see his face that day in the
council when the vote was given! He had
ever made sure that the choice would fall
on him; and when he heard thy name
given forth in place of his, St Hubert!
how he raged! "Mine own esquire, a
threadbare Swiss who hath stood at my
back as I sat at meat, to be preferred to
me!" and with that he ground his teeth,
as if he could have torn thee limb from
limb. I tell thee, kinsman, it was well
worth fifty gold ducats to see and hear
him in his mood that day!'

And he laughed without stint at the discomfiture of the haughty king, whose ever-growing arrogance and insolent disregard of his neighbour's rights and feelings were fast making him as universally hated as he had once been popular. But Rudolf's face showed that *he* was in no laughing mood.

'So be it,' said he at last, with a stern calmness more ominous than the loudest anger; 'it may be that, with God's help, this "threadbare Swiss" will, for all his bluster, be a match for him yet.'

Hardly had he spoken, when a trumpet-blast came echoing from the ramparts of the besieged town, sounding the usual signal for a parley; and a few moments later (to the undisguised amusement of the burg-graf) Rudolf's red-haired henchman, Andrer-Knecht, came to report that the besieged were asking a safe-conduct for one of their officers, sent as an envoy by the prince-bishop to treat for the surrender of the place !

'Meseems, kinsman,' chuckled Hohen-zollern, 'thou hast won the town with a trumpet-blast, like the good knight Sir Joshua in Holy Writ. Thy mere threat hath sufficed to overthrow the walls of Basel.'

In fact, the worthy bishop had been so

frightened by his spy's report that Rudolf's
threats were hardly needed to make him
give way at once. And well might it be
so; for the trembling messenger had faltered
out that Rudolf was the kaiser-elect; that
his kinsman the burg-graf had just come
up with a fresh army (!) to aid the siege;
that he had himself seen Friedrich and his
knights do homage to the new emperor;
and that the latter had sworn, if the town
were not yielded at once, to storm it, burn
it to the ground, and murder every soul
within. He added, by way of rounding off
his story nicely, that the prince-bishop himself was to be hung to the tower of the
cathedral!

This was more than enough for the swag-
gering churchman, who, judging of others
by himself, thought Rudolf quite capable
of such an atrocity. It was one thing for
him to bully a man who seemed weaker
than himself, and quite another thing to
defy an offended kaiser with the whole might
of the empire at his back.

The cowed blusterer lost no time in opening his gates and begging for mercy; and
ere the night was past, he had bound himself
by a solemn oath (which he actually kept
for once) to make full and prompt atone-

ment for those high-handed outrages on the peasantry of the Hapsburg estates which had been Rudolf's original cause of quarrel with him.

'This is the kaiser for whom we have been waiting,' said the Rhineland folk gleefully to each other, when the news of all these things got abroad; 'for the first deed of his reign hath been a deed of mercy, and the second a deed of justice.'

CHAPTER XX.

FLUNG OVER A PRECIPICE.

AS the sun was setting on the third evening after the surrender of Basel, a
small party of well-armed horsemen came
slowly along the narrow, winding path that
zigzagged down the steep and craggy side of
one of that endless procession of wooded
hills from which Northern Switzerland over-
looks the westward sweep of the Rhine.

It was a strange place to meet horsemen,
on that slippery rock-ledge where but one
man could pass at a time, and where one
false step would have been instant death.
But these bold riders moved as fearlessly as
if on a level plain; and their leader seemed
to know his way amid these pathless woods
and dizzy precipices as if he had been familiar
with them all his life. And so he had, in
truth; for he was no other than the new
emperor, Rudolf of Hapsburg.

His cousin Friedrich's warning of King
Ottocar's ill-will had not been lost on the
shrewd young kaiser, who knew the king

well enough to be sure that this ill-will would
speedily vent itself in open attack; and, with
his wonted prompt energy, he resolved to
meet it by striking the first blow.

It was at midnight that he had received
the prince-bishop's submission; and by dawn
he was on his march eastward, the main
army taking the river-road under the command of Friedrich of Hohenzollern, while
Rudolf himself, with a chosen band of
knights, made a short cut through the hills
to stir up the stout Swiss of the Cantons
of Zürich and Thurgau.

To these (many of whom knew him per-
sonally, and all by name) he brought the
first news of his election as emperor; and
the moment they heard it, one and all vowed
to stand by him with every man they could
raise, and at once set about mustering their
forces.

Leaving them instructions to join him as
they could, Rudolf had hurried off again, and
was now nearing the place where he had
arranged to rejoin his army on its march at
the foot of these very hills.   Silent and
thoughtful, he rode on down the endless
zigzags of the mountain path, while the
sinking sun cast a glory around his polished
helmet and set, stern face, as if crowning

him with the imperial crown that he had so suddenly and strangely won.

Well might he look so grave; for he had many and weighty cares on his mind just then. He needed no one to tell him how hard a task he had undertaken by accepting this new dignity. The common people, indeed, would hail with joy any ruler who could free them from the lawless tyranny under which they were groaning; but the robber-barons of the Rhine, the turbulent nobles of Bohemia, and all the countless others who profited by the present misrule, would be against him to a man.

With a leader like Ottocar at its head, such a confederacy might well be too strong for him; and no one knew better than he that, were he worsted in this first trial of strength, his power and dignity as emperor would not be worth a straw. In the bitterness of that galling thought, he uttered half-aloud the famous words that another great ruler was to repeat, in a like case, three centuries later, 'Happier is he that herdeth swine, than he who ruleth an empire!'

'Marry, thou art in the right on't there, my lord,' growled Andrer-Knecht, whose bull-dog attachment to the leader who had (as he often said) 'made him a man,' rejoiced

with his master's joy, and grieved with his
master's grief. 'Both alike are set to make
beasts behave as men, and I trow that is no
easy task.'

'Say'st thou so?' quoth the emperor,
smiling in spite of himself.

'Aye, that do I,' said the henchman,
whom, after all these years of peril and
hardship endured together, Rudolf treated
more as a friend than as a servant. 'For
what was I outlawed and doomed to die,
but for doing what these same well-born
and illustrious thieves, who call themselves
nobles of the empire, do every day—aye,
and boast of it too! My lord Baron Cut-
throat and Sir Count Pick-purse strip an
honest burgher on the high-road of all that
he hath: "Well speed thee, good Sir Knight!
for what were such base churls made, but to
be plundered by gentle-folk?" I, mayhap,
take three pennies from a fat trader at the
corner of a wood: "Fie, the vile thief; away
with him to the gallows!"'

'It is but too true,' said Rudolf, with a
deep sigh.

'Nay, sigh not, since Heaven hath raised
thee up to amend such wrong-doing,' said
his follower bluntly; 'and thou *wilt* amend
it, I wot well. Hark ye, my lord; if thou

wilt walk by my counsel, put no trust in these double-faced nobles, who give you one hand in pledge of good faith, and stab you in the back with the other. Go thou to the peasant and the craftsman, and say thus, " Hans, good fellow, be but loyal to me, and none shall rob thee or make thee afraid !" I trow, when Hans heareth that word, he will fight for thee while he hath breath ; and, trust me, he will strike as stoutly as any of these thieving, reiving, man-devouring knights of the most holy Order of Satan, on whom may——' Here the worthy ex-robber became too unprintably emphatic for quotation.

But ere Hapsburg could reply to this outburst, a sudden clash of steel was heard below, mingled with cries for help, and a hoarse clamour of savage threats and brutal curses.

'Aha !' cried the ex-brigand, pricking up his ears at the familiar sound, 'methinks some one here hath taken up my cast-off trade of robber !'

Sure enough, as they came round a projecting angle of the cliff, they saw far below, just where the path made one of its sharpest turns, a tall man, with his back to a rock, defending himself as best he might against

five savage-looking fellows, who seemed to
be pressing him hard.   Luckily for him, they
could only come at him one at a time on
that narrow path ; but the hindmost of the
gang were already picking up stones to hurl
at their intended victim, who, seeming to
have had quite enough of this unequal
combat, called out to them in a cry-mercy
kind of tone, 'I have done what I could to
defend my charge ; but if ye must needs
have it or my life, take it, and a plague on
ye all !'

So saying, he let fall a heavy bag that
hung at his girdle, which chinked and rattled
as if filled with coin.   The robbers darted at
it like hungry wolves ; but the wily traveller
had, as if by accident, dropped it on the
very brink of the precipice, over which it
toppled at once, to fall with a loud metallic
jingle on the level turf of the valley, fifty
feet below.

Instantly the thieves, troubling themselves
no more about him, went dashing down the
steep, winding path at a break-neck pace,
each eager to be the first to clutch this
precious spoil.

Meanwhile Rudolf and his knights were
hastening to the rescue as fast as the perilous descent would let them ; and, on reach-

ing the spot, they found the plundered man leaning back against the rock in a convulsion of violent though subdued laughter.

'How now, friend?' said the wondering Rudolf; 'thou seem'st right merry for one who hath just been robbed.'

At the sound of his voice the stranger started, and raised his head quickly, revealing a face which, though Rudolf had not seen it for years, had once been too familiar not to be recognised at a glance. 'Hans Bendix, as I live!' cried he joyfully.

'Well met, your Worship,' said Bendix; 'or,' he added, sinking his voice, 'should I not rather say "your Majesty"?'

'Ha!' cried Rudolf, 'how knowest thou that? But of this hereafter; it behoves me now to save thy having' (property) 'from the claws of yon rascals.'

'Trouble not thyself for that, lord kaiser,' said Hans with a broad grin; 'for yon bag of mine, though it jingles blithely, holdeth nought save a handful of copper pence, and my gold is here, safe!'

A burst of angry cries from below confirmed his words, showing that the robbers had found out the trick. But their savage cries and curses ended in a howl of terror as a ringing trumpet-blast awoke all the

echoes of the surrounding hills, and out from
a narrow pass just beyond the bandits came
marching with measured tramp rank after
rank of spearmen (the vanguard of Rudolf's
army) completely barring their way.

Thus hemmed in, between the advancing
host on one side and Hapsburg's descending
train on the other, the brigands were fairly
caught; and, seeing that there was no escape,
they stood sullenly awaiting their doom.

'Here be a sort of thieves quarrelling
over their booty, I trow,' said a deep voice
below. 'Seize them, lads, and bind them;
they shall try ere long if their necks be
strong enough to carry away an oak.'

'Is that thou, Cousin Friedrich?' cried
Rudolf from above.

'It is I, kinsman, and I have this day
been as good a bird-catcher as Kaiser Hein-
rich the Fowler himself, for I have here
snared five goodly carrion crows as ever
perched on a dead horse!'

'Hold them fast! I come!' called out
Rudolf. 'Mount behind me, Bendix.'

'I thank thee, lord kaiser,' said the ex-
shepherd, springing nimbly up. 'I' faith,
when I trudged afoot after my master the
abbot's flocks, little deemed I that I should
ever ride on the same horse with an emperor!'

'He who truly serveth God, and honestly doeth his duty to man,' said Rudolf gravely, 'is worthy not only to ride on an emperor's horse, but to be an emperor himself.'

'And that, I trow, is why they chose *thee*,' rejoined Hans bluntly.

The compliment was so evidently sincere and straight from the heart that it pleased Rudolf more than the most eloquent flattery. But he had no time to reply ere they reached the valley, where he and his cousin greeted each other heartily, while the soldiers shouted in joyful chorus, 'Long live our good Kaiser Rudolf!'

At the word 'kaiser,' the captive robbers started visibly, and looked inquiringly at the young Hapsburg.

'I am the kaiser,' said Rudolf, answering the look. 'Have ye aught of excuse to plead, that I should not doom ye to die?'

'Nought,' replied one who seemed to be the leader, in a tone of sullen resignation. 'What boots it to plead, when we are taken red-handed in the fact? All we ask is a speedy death, and no torture.'

'Torture?' echoed Rudolf, frowning; 'so help me God, no man in German land shall have that to fear, while I sit on the kaiser's throne. Full and fair justice shall

ye have, be assured of that. Now, here
standeth the free man of Richenau, Hans
Bendix, who hath just been robbed, and the
good knight Sir Andrer-Knecht, who hath
himself been a robber; and better judges in
a case of robbery can no man find. How
say ye, good men and true? Be these five
men guilty or no?'

'Guilty! Their own mouth hath spoken
it,' replied the two ready-made judges with
one voice.

'Good,' said the emperor; 'it is for ye
two, then, to pronounce their doom.'

'An't please ye, lord kaiser,' said Hans
bluntly, 'these men did but rob me of a
few pence, which I would gladly have made
over to them in free gift, rather than need
should drive them to thieving. When once
a man's life is taken (as my lord the abbot
was wont to tell us), he who took it can
never put it back, even if he would; wherefore I would fain have thee spare them, if
spared they may be.'

'And I,' added Andrer-Knecht, 'have
been a thief like them, as thou, my lord,
hast said; and it was but by God's mercy
and thine that I was saved from the gallows,
and spared to amend mine ill life somewhat.
Therefore I crave this boom of thee, that I

may have these five men to serve in my troop as soldiers, and atone by good service for what they have done amiss; and if they be again found offending, I promise thee they shall have short and sharp justice.'

'So be it,' said the kaiser. 'How say ye, fellows; are ye willing to accept of my mercy on these terms?'

The reply of the astounded robbers (thus snatched from what they thought certain death) may be easily guessed; and, half an hour later, they were marching away mechanically, like men in a dream, in the ranks of their new comrades.

'And now, friend Hans,' said the emperor to Bendix (who, having been supplied with a horse, rode by his side as they moved on once more), 'I would fain know how thou hast learned that I am chosen kaiser, for I deemed it a secret to all in these parts, save those to whom I have told it.'

'Marry, that is soon told,' said the ex-shepherd, whom Rudolf's kindly tone and manner, and his own former acquaintance with him, had put more at his ease than most men of his class would have been, in that age, in the presence of a real live emperor. 'Some seven nights agone, there came to our abbey of Reichenau two heralds

from Frankfort; and to my charge it fell
to entertain them, as being my lord abbot's
steward.'

'Steward, say'st thou?' echoed Rudolf.
'I wish thee joy, then, comrade, of thy
preferment; and in truth thou hast well
earned it, having once saved thy master
from the wrath of King Ottocar himself.'

Bendix chuckled hoarsely at this allusion
to his old exploit, which was by this time
a standard tale through all the Rhine-land,
and had been wrought by a wandering
minstrel into a universally popular ballad,
some fragments of which still exist.

'They set forth again on the morrow,' he
went on, 'along the north side of the Rhine;
but being both of them leaky casks, and
having, it may be, partaken over-freely of
my master's good wine, they let fall, ere
they left, as much of their errand as made
it no hard task for me to guess what was
left untold.'

'Aye,' said Rudolf with stern contempt,
'by such fools are the secrets of kings and
kaisers betrayed. Well?'

'Both were seeking thee,' pursued Hans;
'the one being sent by the great council to
bring thee word that thou wert chosen
kaiser, and the other by King Ottocar, in

the first heat of his wrath at not being chosen himself, to defy thee, and refuse to do thee homage for his territories in Austria, of which he hath made himself duke (as thou knowest) by sacred right of fist and sword; for I wot not of any other right that he hath.'

'I *do* know it,' said the young kaiser with grim emphasis.

Then broke suddenly over his set, stern face the light of a great resolution—such a light as more than one of those who rode near him then were to see on that face once more, in the hour of his last and mightiest conflict.

'Hans Bendix,' said he, 'I have somewhat to say to thee, knowing that thou art to be trusted. Give me thy counsel on a certain matter, and spare not to speak it plainly; for thou speak'st not to the Kaiser of the Empire, but to thine old friend and fellow-soldier, Rudolf of Hapsburg!'

'So help me all the holy saints,' cried Hans, whose rough face lighted up at the last words, 'if speech or deed of mine can profit thee, I am thy man to the death!'

'That I know well,' said Rudolf kindly; 'and now hearken. Saidst thou not that yon heralds had taken the north side of the Rhine? Then will Ottocar's message not reach me; and I know that he, having puffed away the first gust of his anger, will wait to see if his bluster hath cowed me, and will thus lose much time. Now, ere he can gather force to stay me, I am minded to march straight on Vienna and take from him these ill-gotten Austrian lands of his; and I would learn of thee, who knowest these countries well, how and by what road my march should be.'

'A good thought!' cried Bendix, who had listened with an ever-broadening grin of wondering delight; '"fresh fish are good fish," as our proverb says. Take thy way, then, through the mountains of the Tyrol; for so will Ottocar have less chance to hear of thy march, and also thou shalt thus win many men to thee. Since the last Duke of Meran was murdered, five-and-twenty years ago, the headship of the realm hath gone a-begging, and all is as it were a Christmas scramble for apples, each snatching what he can; and many know not to whom they belong, and some belong to no man at all. All honest folk are well a-weary of such disorders, and would fain have a lawful head; and also they be ill pleased that King Ottocar is for lording it over them in virtue of the title that he hath *not* got to be Duke of Austria. When they hear thy trumpets sound, I'll gage my steward's chain against a rotten stirrup-leather that they will one and all stand by thee to the death!'

Rudolf at once took this good advice, and followed it out like the great general that he was. Knowing that he had no resistance to fear yet, he broke up his army into three or four small detachments, which, marching by different routes, might easily be mistaken by any spy of Ottocar for the straggling bands of German soldiers-of-fortune then flocking to the wars of Northern Italy.

Crossing the Rhine near Feldkirch, Rudolf plunged into the fragrant shadow of the great Tyrolese pine-forests—saw the bare white scalp of the Gross-Glockner towering above the rolling clouds twelve thousand feet overhead—passed the rushing Drave, as it came foaming and leaping down from its lonely ice-field—and marched on through the stern grandeur of the Puster-Thal, little dreaming that, in this same valley, a train of horseless coaches, moved by vapour, would fly in an hour over the distance that took him a whole day to cover.

As he advanced, his army grew like a rolling snowball. At the very name of the good kaiser who came to beat down violence and maintain law, the free burghers of the towns girt on their swords, the hunter took down spear and crossbow, the peasant caught up wood-knife and axe; and while King Ottocar, in his palace at Prag, was sneering at the 'threadbare Swiss lackey' of an emperor, that threadbare Swiss was almost in sight of Vienna, with fifteen thousand men at his back!

The weather favoured the bold invader like all else, for, though the nights were already beginning to be cold, the days were still fine and bright; and so clear was the air that, when they looked down from the last ridge of the Simmering Pass on the great plain of the Danube, the towers and steeples of Vienna were plainly visible far away to the north.

As the young emperor stood gazing in thoughtful silence at the distant capital, from the shadowy thickets behind him broke a wild and haggard form clothed in rags, evidently one of the forest-solitaries, half-hermit, and half-madman, so abundant in that age. 'Go forward to the city!' he cried shrilly, as he clutched Rudolf's arm with one hand and pointed to Vienna with the other. 'Go! beneath yon walls profit and peril await thee!'

And the prophet vanished as if the earth had swallowed him.

CHAPTER XXI.

A MIDNIGHT BLAZE.

IT was the morning of Christmas Eve, but such a Christmas Eve as few of the oldest inhabitants of Vienna could remember.

The winter had been unusually mild and backward; and in place of the clear sky and hard frost which the Viennese were wont to associate with their great winter festival, a damp white mist brooded over the valley of the Danube, so thick that the solitary man who was making his way slowly to the south-east over the great plain was forced to pick his way almost as carefully as if it were midnight.

But all at once he stopped short, and bent his head forward to listen, as if he had heard some warning sound in front of him; and just as he did so, a trumpet-blast rang out through the mist, seemingly but a little way ahead.

The listener started slightly, and muttered with an air of relief, 'Aha! if my memory serve me right, I have heard yon trumpet-call before; and if it be as I think, this is

a piece of luck worth all the gold of Ind.'
So saying, forward he went as fast as the
mist would let him.

'Stand! Who goes there?' called a deep
voice from the depth of the chill white cloud.

'How now, Karl Sprenger, is it thou?'
cried the stranger, who seemed to know the
voice.

'What! My old comrade, Hans Bendix?'
shouted the unseen sentinel gleefully. 'What
brings thee here, lad, wandering about like
a spectre in this plaguy mist? But be that
as it may, I am blithe to see thee again;
it is long since we met.' And a huge
figure, issuing from the cloud, grasped
Bendix's hand with rough cordiality.

'Art thou still with Sir Conrad of
Hohenzollern?' asked Hans eagerly.

'Aye, surely. With whom else? I trow
he will be right glad to see thee.'

'Bring me to him straightway,' said the
other hastily; 'every moment now is worth
gold.'

A few moments later he stood before the
leader of the detachment.

Conrad was less changed than his visitor
had expected. The fresh, smooth beauty
of the boy had indeed matured into the
grave and stately dignity of the man; but

his handsome face wore the same bright, fearless, self-reliant look as ever—the look of one who was prepared for all perils, but feared none.

'Pardon me if I greet thee somewhat hastily, my lord,' said Hans quickly, but there is no time to lose if thou wouldst do a priceless service to thy kinsman, Kaiser Rudolf.'

And then he told his wondering hearer, as briefly and clearly as he could, that King Ottocar had flatly refused to do homage to Rudolf as emperor, or to give up the Austrian territories that he had unjustly seized; that the emperor had made a forced march through the Tyrol to take him by surprise, and was now at hand with his whole army; and that it was of vital importance, ere the garrison of Vienna could be strengthened, to capture the city and make it a base of operations for the reduction of the other towns held by Ottocar's soldiers in the Duchy of Austria.

'And now, Sir Conrad,' he ended, 'thou hast here, they tell me, a hundred stout fellows, and in the city itself the kaiser hath friends not a few, as mine own eyes have seen. I ask thee then, as knight and Christian, wilt thou aid me to do manful service to our kaiser, who is thine own kinsman and friend?'

'That will I, right blithely,' said Hohenzollern, with all his wonted heartiness; 'and, with God's blessing and thy shrewd wit to speed us. I nothing doubt but we shall succeed. Tell me thy plan, then, good fellow, and be assured that nought which I can do shall be lacking to further it.'

The answer came in a few whispered words, which, whatever they were, made Conrad's face grow radiant as he listened. 'On my faith, friend Hans, thou art a born general,' cried he joyfully. 'As thou sayest, so shall it be; and I will straightway send off a swift rider to bid my cousin the kaiser hasten hither with as many men as he can bring. Rare sport will it be, I trow, if, when he cometh to Vienna gate, he shall find it opened to him by *us*!'

'Goodly work this for bearded men, to stand and stare at these spiritless churls driving their fellow-asses to market! Marry, if we were set to fire their homesteads, and plunder their barns, and drive off their cattle, it would be better sport, I wot! May the saints send us some fighting ere long, or we shall all grow mildewed from want of use!'

So growled a big, ruffianly-looking soldier as he stood leaning idly on his spear at the south gate of Vienna, and watched with a coarse sneer the passing stream of carts laden with hay, vegetables, or firewood, the pedlars with their packs, the market-women with their baskets, the strolling minstrels thrumming on their light guitars, and the barefooted peasants trudging behind their laden donkeys, all alike bound for the market that was held that morning in the great square of the town.

There should have been, by rights, a second sentry on the other side of the gate, and half a dozen more soldiers in the guard-room behind, with an officer at their head. But, as usual, long security had relaxed the bonds of discipline, and the second sentry was chiefly conspicuous by his absence, while the guard-room contained no one but the officer himself, who was sleeping off the effects of an extra flask of Rhine wine.

One of the minstrels in the throng (who had got a lift on a hay-cart, from which he leaped nimbly as it halted at the corner of the market-place) had evidently been in the city before, for he seemed to have plenty of chums among the town-folk. To and fro he went through the crowd, saying a word to this man and a word to that, till he had gone the round of the whole market.

Such of the king's soldiers as happened to notice him at all took it for granted, from the impish grin which lighted up his face, that he was cutting jokes on the citizens, after the manner of his class. But, had they watched him more closely, they would have seen that he left grave looks and excited whispers behind him. And well might it be so; for this pretended minstrel was no other than Hans Bendix, and the news he was spreading under this show of jesting was to bear strange fruit ere that day was over.

All at once the seeming minstrel sprang into an empty cart in the centre of the market-place, and, twanging his chords loudly, called to the crowd that instantly began to form round him: 'Worthy sirs, permit a poor lad to do what he can to earn your gracious approval and a new jacket!'

With this broad hint (which was received with general laughter) Hans sang as follows:

'The wolves were left in charge of the sheep,
  And hey! how free they were!
They hunted them down, and stripped off their fleece,
  And the flesh from their bones did tear.

'Then two or three dogs came by that way,
  And they said, "What is this that ye do?
 If ye wolves have nought but teeth for the flock,
  Mayhap we'll have teeth for you!"

'Said the wolves to the dogs, "Nay, we are your
   kin,
  Come and help to devour the flock."
 Said the dogs to the wolves, "We're no kin to
    thieves,
  So beware of an ugly knock!"

'"Oh, help us! help!" cried the sheep in despair;
  Said the dogs, "Be ye all of good cheer!
 There's a shepherd who bears St Rudolf's staff,
  And that shepherd himself is near!"'

The last two lines (on which the singer
laid a peculiar emphasis) produced a general
though carefully repressed excitement in the
listening crowd. But ere the song could
go farther, it was cut short by a trumpet-
blast just outside the town-gate—a coinci-
dence which was recalled later on, though
no one thought anything of it at the time.

The trumpet-call brought out the officer
of the gate, who had by this time slept
himself sober enough to attend to his duty;
and he hurried forward to inspect and challenge the armed force that waited outside,
which was neither more nor less than

Conrad of Hohenzollern's hundred men-at-arms, with himself at their head.

But Conrad had had the sense to follow the wise counsel of Bendix, who shrewdly calculated that if Hohenzollern, well known as a cousin and friend of the new emperor, were to present himself before a town held by the soldiers of that emperor's declared enemy, he would either be shut out of it as a foe or shut into it as a prisoner and a hostage. He had therefore advised Conrad to roll up his tell-tale banner, put his lieutenant in command of the party, and assume the character of the latter's esquire.

All this was done, and with the best possible result; for the Bohemian officer no sooner heard that these soldiers were King Ottocar's liegemen, led by Sir Max von Faustrecht, and just returned from an expedition on the king's service (as was really the case) among the Transylvanian mountains, than he began to congratulate himself on this accession to the strength of the garrison, and at once let them pass in.

Keeping his men well together, Sir Max rode on to the market-place. Halting by the great fountain, he ordered his trumpet to sound, and then, standing up in his stirrups, shouted with a well-assumed show

of fierceness: 'In the king's name, I demand
quarters for myself and my men. Where
be these dogs of guild-masters? Let them
come hither quickly, and listen to my
orders.'

The heads of the various trade-guilds,
already apprised by Hans of what was to
come, drew near at this rough summons
with rueful faces, and an admirably feigned
air of terrified submission.

Then Von Faustrecht, after bespattering
them all with a few choice terms of speech
(such as King Ottocar's captains were wont
to fling about pretty freely) ordered Gottfried Stein to give lodging to his 'esquire'
(Conrad of Hohenzollern) and twenty of
the soldiers, as head of the bakers' guild.
He billeted twenty more on Karl Fleischer,
the head of the butchers' guild; the guild-
masters of the curriers and the cutlers were
also saddled with a score apiece; and the
remaining twenty, with Sir Max himself,
quartered themselves on the chief of the
clothiers' guild.

In a very few minutes the whole matter
was settled; and the sharpest of the
Bohemian soldiers who were looking on and
listening had not the least idea that, under
their very eyes, all was being prepared for

the overpowering of their garrison and the capture of the town!

But these confident gentlemen might have felt less secure, had they overheard the talk which passed that evening between Hohenzollern and his host, whose house and bakery stood close to the citadel that overawed the central part of the town.

'For the soldiers in the town I care nought,' said Conrad; 'for, scattered as they are, and careless from over-confidence, they will be but a mouthful for the stout lads of the guilds, with my trusty men-at-arms to aid them. But this citadel' (and he glanced meaningly at the huge dark tower that loomed above them against the star-lit sky) 'is strong and well-manned, and will be a hard nut to crack; nor know I of any device whereby we may win it without bloodshed.'

'Methinks *I* do,' said the sturdy baker, with a gruff chuckle. 'Hearken to my plan, noble sir, and see how it pleaseth you.'

A whisper, as low as if he feared that the very walls might hear him, conveyed Stein's project, which seemed to startle even the cool Conrad.

'Wilt thou really do this?' cried he. 'Bethink thee, it is all thou hast.'

'Were it more,' said the brave man firmly, 'I would gladly give it all for the good cause.'

'Give me thy hand, good friend,' cried Conrad with a glowing face. 'Thou art the bravest of us all, and may God requite thee according to thy merits; but be assured that my kinsman the emperor and I will see to it that thou be no penny the worse for that which thou doest for our cause. Methinks a kaiser who hath hearts like thine to rely on, is mightier than if his cause were championed by all the armies of Christendom!'

Two hours later the baker Stein, having got his guests and all his household out of harm's way, deliberately set fire to his own house in three places at once.

'Fire! Fire! Help, comrades, help!'

'The tower is all aflame! Water, water, quickly!'

'Ho there, knaves! Will ye let the fire devour us all? Bestir ye, or we are but lost men!'

'Yon dog of a baker hath overheated his oven, belike, for 'tis from his house that the flame cometh. Would he were in the midst of it, he and all his household!'

So shouted the officers and soldiers of

the citadel garrison, as they flew wildly to
and fro; but their frantic activity came too
late. The brave burgher had not made his
heroic sacrifice in vain. The flames kindled
by his own hand to destroy his only shelter
had caught the hated tower as he intended,
and had by this time got such a hold upon
it as to defy all efforts to quench them;
and ere long the dreaded stronghold was
all one red and roaring blaze.

The glare of the flames, the furious clang-
ing of the alarm-bell, and the general
uproar that followed startled the Bohemian
soldiers quartered in the town, who came
pouring out pell-mell, in utter disorder, only
to be at once assailed and overpowered by
the armed citizens, against whom they had
no chance in those narrow, crooked streets,
blocked with carts and wagons; and they
were all made prisoners without the loss of
a single life.

Meanwhile a lance-prisade (corporal) and
four men from Conrad's band presented
themselves at the south gate as if to re-
lieve the sentry, whom they seized, gagged,
and bound ere he could utter a cry, and
then opened the gate to a strong force of
cavalry that seemed to have been waiting
outside.

In trooped the horsemen forthwith, and
at their head rode the Emperor Rudolf
himself in full armour, with his banner
waving over his head, and his inseparable
Andrer-Knecht at his side as usual.

The trumpet-blast which told that the
kaiser himself was in the city was like
the voice of doom to the panic-stricken
garrison of the citadel, who had just been
driven headlong out of it by the flames,
without armour and almost without arms.
Nothing doubting that the emperor would
celebrate his victory, after the fashion of
the good old times, by hanging them all on
the spot, they threw down what weapons
they had, and cried for mercy.

In a word, they were all made prisoners
without striking a blow, and handed over
to the charge of the staunch master-baker,
Gottfried Stein, whom the emperor honoured and rewarded as he deserved on
learning what he had done; and when, just
as day was beginning to break, the main
body of Rudolf's army came up to the city-
gate in turn, after marching all night, they
found the first Hapsburg kaiser as completely master of his future capital as he
had ever been of his own ancestral castle.

CHAPTER XXII.

THE FALL OF A CURTAIN.

THE news of Rudolf's capture of Vienna ran through all Austria like wild-fire; and the moment it became known that there really was a lawful emperor at last, and that he was actually among them to repress violence and to maintain justice, the people (as Andrer-Knecht and Bendix had foretold) rose on his side as one man.

In fact, all alike were eager to shake off the hated yoke of the Bohemian king, who had unjustly seized their country, and held it against their will by foreign soldiers; for as such the Germans regarded the Slavonian Czechs of Bohemia, with whom Ottocar had garrisoned the chief Austrian towns.

But all these garrisons were now of little avail. Some were surprised and overpowered by the townsmen themselves; some, losing heart, made off without waiting to be attacked; and the few that *did* show a bold front were speedily reduced by Rudolf himself, who, leaving his two Hohenzollern cousins to hold Vienna, marched in person with the bulk of his force through the whole Duchy of Austria, carrying all before him.

But, true to his maxim of being just to all, the new emperor sternly forbade all plundering and violence, a proceeding which, after the lawless ways of the king's Bohemian and Thuringian men-at-arms, struck the Austrian farmers and traders as a very great improvement. Nor was he less merciful to the Bohemian soldiers that he made prisoners, who, judging the young kaiser by other generals of his time, expected nothing short of being hanged to the last man from the towers of their captured forts. But Rudolf sent them home unharmed, telling them that he had no quarrel with men who had but obeyed their master's orders.

'This is the kaiser for my money!' cried a burly peasant in the market-place of Vienna. 'What think ye? My grand-sire, being somewhat tottery with age, slips and falls on the high-road. Comes Kaiser Rudolf on his steed, and sees him there; down leaps he straightway, raises the old man from the earth, asks how he did, lifts him on his own horse (I lie not, as I am Christian man) and leads it right up to our door! Marry, one might have waited long ere yon haughty King Ottocar had done the like!'

'And he kissed my little Gretchen in passing, and called her a goodly child,' said a stout, ruddy market-woman, with a smile of motherly pleasure; 'and the little one smiled and held out her tiny arms to him, as if she knew him for a friend; and I'll warrant she did, too! God bless his kind heart, say I, wherever he may go.'

In a word, every heart in Austria thrilled in response to the stirring words of a sermon preached on the following Sunday in the church of St Stephen at Vienna, to a congregation that crowded the grand old house of prayer to its very doors; and the preacher's text was, 'He hath put down the mighty from their seats, and hath exalted the humble and meek.'

Meanwhile, what was King Ottocar thinking of all this? The fall of Vienna had been a thunderbolt to him; for so well had Rudolf's secret been kept, that the king knew nothing of his march eastward, and thought him still on the Rhine. Ere Ottocar had time to rally from the shock of these evil tidings, came news of town after town yielding or being taken, till the king could not call a foot of land his own in the country where he had so lately been supreme.

In fact, the arrogant monarch, like many other over-confident leaders, had been undone by despising his enemy. That this 'threadbare Swiss lackey' would be able to oppose *him*, this disdainful king had never thought for a moment; and he had looked forward complacently to gathering all his forces, and pulling down this emperor of a day as quickly as he had been set up.

But he had vastly under-rated the soldier-like promptitude of a man with whom to decide and to act were one; and he had also failed to realise the deep and wide-spread discontent aroused by his high-handed arrogance and violent usurpation. Nor had he allowed for the vast addition of strength given to Hapsburg by the mere title of emperor, among men ready to accept any government that could end this riot of lawless oppression.

Anyhow, here was Kaiser Rudolf on the border of Bohemia, with fifty thousand men at his back, and others flocking to him daily; and what was to prevent his marching straight on Prag, and burning King Ottocar's palace over his head ere an army could be raised to repel him?

In fact, the arrogant king found himself fairly overmatched; and, galling as it was to him to have to own it, he had no choice but to yield for the time, in the hope that his turn would come later.

So it befell that, one fine April morning, both banks of the Danube opposite Camberg Islet were crowded like a market. The southern shore was alive with steel caps and spear-points, prancing horses, waving plumes, shining armour, and all the splendour of a well-equipped army. Along the northern bank eddied an excited throng of sun-browned peasants and grimy artisans, kerchiefed women and bare-footed children, monks, pedlars, minstrels, pilgrims, and what not; and all eyes were turned eagerly to the islet, and fixed expectantly on a large tent upon it.

Nor was this excitement to be wondered at; for on that day the king was to pay to Rudolf the homage that he had so long refused; and the people whose land he had over-run were in no mood to spare the haughty tyrant one jot of his well-deserved mortification.

Ottocar had done his best, however, to lighten the bitterness of this crushing blow to his pride, by stipulating that the actual doing of homage should take place in a tent, to which only a chosen few should be admitted; and Rudolf, whose gallant heart was too great for any petty triumph over a fallen foe, understood and agreed.

Presently a shrill trumpet-blast awoke all the echoes; and then came a trampling of hoofs, and a rolling cloud of dust.

'The king! the king!' buzzed through the crowd; and, sure enough, out of the dust-cloud issued a gallant train of horsemen, glittering with embroidery till they fairly dazzled the eyes of the lookers-on, and in the midst rode King Ottocar himself, one blaze of jewels and cloth-of-gold from head to foot.

'I' faith, he hath pranked him out bravely to kneel before his master,' chuckled a sturdy peasant; 'it is as if a man should don his holiday jerkin to be hanged!'

'And lo! here cometh our kaiser in his work-a-day clothes,' put in a second man, with a broad grin. 'He, I trow, needeth none of these May-day fineries to set him off.'

In fact, a boat was just then seen to put off from the south bank, in the stern of which sat Kaiser Rudolf himself, in his dinted armour and well-worn grey riding-cloak.

At the same moment Ottocar's boat glided away from the north shore; and king and kaiser, landing on the islet from opposite sides (each with two attendants) vanished into the tent prepared for them.

And then, all at once (no one knew how) down came the tent-hangings with a run, leaving only the bare poles; and there, in full view of the thousands of watching eyes along both banks, knelt King Ottocar, in his splendid dress, at the feet of the 'threadbare Swiss' whom he had despised! A universal roar of laughter made the air ring; and Ottocar, springing to his feet, and darting a look of fiery hatred at Rudolf (who was quite as much amazed as himself at this strange mischance), rushed away in a frenzy of rage.

But the mishap that was to have such fatal results was really due to the mischievous dexterity of Rudolf's favourite attendant, Andrer-Knecht, who, owing the king a grudge for more than one wanton affront, had purposely hung the tent-curtains in such a way as to fall at the first shake. Little dreamed the reckless jester, as he chuckled over the proud king's humiliation, that that joke was to cost thousands of lives, and his own among the rest.

CHAPTER XXIII.

IT was the morning of 26th August 1278;
and the ramparts of Vienna were one
unbroken line of eager faces, all turned
expectantly toward the great plain of the
Marchfeld, the wide green surface of
which was all alive with waving banners
and gleaming steel, prancing steeds, gay
plumes, shining mail, the leather jackets
of archers, the buff-coats and tall spears
of men-at-arms, and all the stern magni-
ficence of two great armies in battle array.

Well might those eager spectators gaze
so anxiously toward the battlefield; for
upon the struggle about to begin there
hung the fate of their country, and the life
of every soul among the lookers-on.

King Ottocar had never forgiven or forgotten his great humiliation, and he had
now come with the whole strength of his
kingdom to avenge it; and should he gain
the day, it was easy to guess what mercy
he would show to the city that had over-

powered his garrison, supported his enemy, and rejoiced at his disgrace.

Well might the men's brows grow dark, and the women's cheeks turn pale, while muttered prayers, half-stifled by sobs, broke from quivering lips every here and there.

'If yon cruel Ottocar should win,' faltered a pale-faced mother, drawing her children closer to her as she spoke, 'sword and fire will be the word in every street of Vienna. God help us all!'

'There go two words to that bargain,' growled a brawny smith. 'There be as good men here, I trow, as any he brings with him; and ere these out-land dogs play the Saracen in our streets, there shall be crowns cracked some few!'

'See, yonder rides our kaiser; may God fight for him this day!' cried another man, arching one hand over his eyes, while pointing with the other to a solitary figure that had just advanced a few paces in front of the long battle-line of the southern army.

It was indeed Rudolf of Hapsburg, praying his last prayer to the God of battles ere closing with the hosts of the oppressor. The few simple words were barely spoken ere a blast of trumpets made the air ring; there came a mighty shout, a thunder of charging hoofs, and all vanished in a whirl of dust.

For a time nothing could be seen; but at length the rising wind cast aside the dust-cloud, and all eyes could see Rudolf's left wing giving way before the furious charge of the Bohemian knights, who, sweeping on in one vast glittering wave, with Ottocar's banner flaunting over them, burst with a fierce shout on the kaiser's men, and bore them down with irresistible force.

'Heaven have mercy on us!' murmured a woman's voice despairingly.

'Heaven *will* have mercy, my children; fear not!' said a grey-bearded monk firmly. 'See ye not how Heaven itself smiles on your champion, and frowns on your oppressor?'

In fact, while a vast black cloud lowered ominously over Ottocar's charging host, the southern sky was bright and clear, and lighted up Rudolf's army with a glory of unclouded sunshine—a sight that greatly comforted the anxious crowd, whose superstition saw in it a sure token of victory to their beloved kaiser; and, sure enough, the old monk had hardly spoken, when this battle between the hosts of light and darkness (as it really seemed to be) took a new and startling turn.

Rudolf, whose soldier-eye let nothing escape it, had foreseen and provided against an attack on this weak part of his line by posting a chosen body of Swiss archers in a patch of broken and bush-clad ground on his extreme left; and now was the time for them to show what they could do.

As the Bohemian charge came thundering on, there was a sudden twang of bow-strings and a whiz of flying missiles, and the short, strong bolts flew rattling among the charging horsemen with a force that the strongest armour could not resist. Down went horse and man on every side; and their leader himself, Count Mistislav of Nostitz, while cheering on his men, was smitten by a bolt between helmet and gorget, and fell heavily to the earth, a dead man.

'Well aimed, countryman!' said Rudolf to the successful shot, knowing how a soldier values a word of approval from his general. 'There be good marksmen in our Canton of Uri, but I wot thou art the best of all.'

'Not so, lord kaiser,' cried the Swiss, with a pleased smile at being thus coupled

with the emperor himself. 'I have left
a lad at home in Burglen, who is my
master with the arblast' (cross-bow). 'Ask
of the folk in our village who is their best
archer, and I'll warrant they all make
answer that it is my boy Wilhelm Tell.'

The time was to come when the Austrian
nobles, and Rudolf's own son likewise, were
to hear more than enough of the archery
of that obscure lad in Burglen. But all
this was still in the unknown future, and
just then the Emperor Rudolf had something else to think of.

Putting himself at the head of a fresh
body of horse, which he had kept in reserve,
he made a rapid wheel to the left, and,
falling on the flank of the Bohemians, who
were disordered by the shower of bolts and
the fall of their leader, he rode them down
and swept them away like dust, and completely restored the fortune of the battle
in that quarter.

Meanwhile, on his right (where Conrad
of Hohenzollern was in command, with his
kinsman Friedrich as his lieutenant) the fight
was pretty evenly balanced, neither side
being able to gain any decisive advantage
over the other. But the real tug of battle
was in the centre, where King Ottocar and

his guards, the veterans of a hundred fights, were bearing down all before them.

The first shock of his onset had fallen on the vassals of the Abbot of Reichenau, at whose head was the steward, Hans Bendix himself. The brave fellows stood to it as stoutly as men could do; but against the resistless charge of the steel-clad horsemen (who then formed the main strength of every army) foot-soldiers had little chance at best, and, do what they would, they were broken and driven back,

Bendix, who had perilled himself as fearlessly as if he bore a charmed life, strove manfully to rally them, but in vain. Twice was he struck down, and twice did he struggle to his feet again; but the third time a terrific mace-stroke beat him down to the earth as if crushed by a falling mountain, and he moved no more.

The disorder spread, and the whole centre was just giving way, when a shout of 'Hapsburg to the rescue!' rose clear and high above the din, and in came Rudolf and his victorious cavalry. The rout was instantly checked; the assailants were charged and broken in turn; and Rudolf, rising in his stirrups, was waving on his men to victory, when through the whirling dust in front of him, not a spear-length away, broke a well-remembered figure.

It was the terrible Count Valens of Thuringia himself, with not a few tell-tale streaks of grey in his bushy red beard, and many more crimes as well as years on his head, but still as fierce and untamable as ever. 'How now, boy, art thou so brisk?' cried he jeeringly. 'Stand still a moment, that I may bear thee away on my lance-point, as a toy at a village fair.'

As the coarse taunt was uttered, Rudolf's noble steed sank mortally wounded by the Thuringian's lance, horse and man going down together.

One moment more and the Hapsburg dynasty would have ended ere it had well begun. But, just in the nick of time, Andrer-Knecht (at his master's side as usual) thrust himself between, and fell dead beneath the blow aimed at Rudolf.

But he did not die in vain. Rudolf had fallen clear of his wounded horse, and sprang to his feet once more, just in time to meet the count's renewed attack. Furious at his trusty servant's fall, he beat aside Valens's lifted weapon, and threw all his strength into one mighty blow, which went down through helmet and head to the very teeth.

With Valens died the courage of his followers, who gave way on every side; and victory seemed already within the emperor's grasp, when (as if these strange turns of fortune were never to end) King Ottocar himself, having routed the troops with which Conrad of Hohenzollern strove gallantly to bar his way, came like a thunderbolt on Rudolf's disordered squadrons, with the best of his knights at his back.

At the cry of 'The king! the king!' Rudolf (who had mounted the slain count's horse instead of his own) wheeled at once to meet this new foe, and the two great captains came face to face at last.

'I see the man!' roared Ottocar as he recognised the emperor, unconsciously repeating the words uttered by another bold leader in like circumstances seventeen centuries before; and he *flew* like a roused *lion* at the hated 'Swiss lackey' to whom he owed the bitterest memory of his whole life.

The two men met like conflicting whirlwinds; and, as often happened in that age of personal prowess, the soldiers on either side suspended their own conflict as if by tacit consent to watch the encounter of their leaders.

For a moment or two nothing could be

seen of the combatants, though from the
billowy dust-cloud that enfolded them came
a ceaseless clang of heavy blows, a fierce
snorting, and a dull trampling of hoofs; and
then, as the whirling dust began to subside,
the anxious watchers beheld the mighty
Ottocar lying dead on the trampled earth,
while over him stood Rudolf, with the glow
of triumph on his noble face softened by a
thrill of regretful pity for his old general
and fellow-crusader, who had indeed (as
Mad Matthew's dying words foretold) been
ruined by his own jealousy and pride.

Ottocar's death ended the battle at one
blow. The foot-soldiers flung away their
weapons, the horsemen turned their steeds
to fly. The great array melted away like
mist; and the watching citizens of Vienna
drew a deep breath of relief, and gave
thanks to God that the reign of violence
was over.

The after fortunes of Rudolf of Hapsburg
and his descendants are written in history,
and every schoolboy knows how worthily
the great leader wore the imperial crown
that he had so bravely won. But to
the last day of his life he never forgot the
moderation and justice that had been the
guiding principles of his whole career; and

when he died, in the nineteenth year of
his reign, the love and regret of an entire
nation followed 'the good Kaiser' to his
grave.

How the House of Hohenzollern struggled
onward through long centuries of ceaseless
effort, and countless strange alternations of
good and evil fortune to world-wide fame
and the headship of all Germany, the
ablest biographer of Frederick the Great has
told in words that can never die. But there
was no prophet then to forewarn Conrad of
Hohenzollern and Rudolf of Hapsburg, as
they grasped each other's hands like brothers
on the field of their greatest victory, that
the House of Hapsburg would in after times
convulse all Europe with a seven years'
war, the sole object of which was to crush
the House of Hohenzollern; and that this
same Marchfeld that had just witnessed
Rudolf's crowning triumph, was one day
to see the pride of his descendant dashed
down in the dust by the thunder-stroke of
Napoleon. And now both Houses have
fallen!

Andrer-Knecht was buried in St Stephen's
Church at Vienna, with all the honour due
to one who had indeed been 'faithful to
the death.' The kaiser himself was among

those who bore him to the grave; and on his tomb the master whom he had died to save placed a very appropriate epitaph:

> *Greater love hath no man than this, that*
> *a man lay down his life for his friends.*

Hans Bendix recovered from his wound, in spite of the blundering of three doctors; and, his master the abbot being now dead, he accepted, at the emperor's special request, an important post at the imperial court, where his native shrewdness and sound common-sense more than once did the kaiser good service. Many of the good sayings for which he was famous were quoted by the people long after his death; and to this day one may hear at times, in some quiet little German village, the racy old ballad which tells how Hans's keen mother-wit once got the better of the great King of Bohemia himself.

THE END.